PELOT
Pelot, Mayi,
Memories of tomorrow /

MEMORIES OF TOMORROW

Heirloom Books Series

It Walks in Beauty
by Chandler Davis

Dorothea Dreams
by Suzy McKee Charnas

New Amazonia
by Elizabeth Burgoyne Corbett

The Merril Theory of Lit'ry Criticism
by Judith Merril

Ring of Swords
by Eleanor Arnason

Memories of Tomorrow
by Mayi Pelot

About the Aqueduct Press
Heirloom Books

Aqueduct Press's series of Heirloom Books aims to bring back into print and preserve work that has helped make feminist science fiction what it is today—work that though clearly of its time is still pleasurable to read, work that is thought-provoking, work that can still speak powerfully to readers. The series takes its name from the seeds of older strains of vegetables, so valuable and in danger of being lost. Our hope is to keep these books from being lost, as works that do not make it into the canon so often are.

~L. Timmel Duchamp

Heirloom Series

Number 6

Memories of Tomorrow

by
Mayi Pelot

translated by
Arrate Hidalgo

Published by Aqueduct Press
PO Box 95787
Seattle, WA 98145-2787
www.aqueductpress.com

ISBN: 978-1-61976-226-8
Library of Congress Control Number: 2021952097

Cover photographs copyright © 2022 Silvia Calleja
Interior illustrations copyright © Irene Borda

 ETXEPARE
EUSKAL
INSTITUTUA
The translation of this book has been
subsidized by the Etxepare Basque Institute

Printed in the USA by McNaugton & Gunn

To Txomin Peillen
and also
to a spider
gifted with cunning

Contents

Translator's Foreword

MAYI PELOT WAS an innovator, in more than one sense. This is something I began to realise years ago, when I first came across her work in my attempts to locate whatever heritage there was in terms of Basque speculation. And the range of Pelot's innovation soon grew before me as I delved deeper into her imagination as well as into her forging new forms of expression in the Basque language itself.

It has been thanks to the opportunity to translate these short stories that I have come to understand the dimensions of her expansive, playful attitude towards the way words form and interact in Basque. It has often been mentioned about her that she was a newcomer to the language she wrote in (not unlike me, she began to use Basque as a medium for living in her twenties), and that she wrote science fiction, at that. Northern Basque Country author and queer literary icon Itxaro Borda has talked about unified Basque or *euskara batua*—the standardized variety of the language now used in media, government and education—in the context in which Pelot was writing, pointing out that it was considered metallic, technical, even science fictional. But, as Borda notes, in contrast to the style favoured by the wave of social commentary in which she developed as an author, Pelot was in search of a different kind of Basque to that used by her contemporaries, and she found it by creating her own kind, one on which her worlds could find solid ground.

Borda once mentioned to me, in fact, that back in the 1980s technical dictionaries did not exist yet for Basque. And so Pelot took advantage of the language's fondness for compounding, not only to name imaginary devices, but also to provide alternatives to the many words being imported into Basque—mainly from English—for existing technology. My translation decisions around this aspect of Pelot's work can be roughly divided into three groups, which I will briefly describe below.

The first includes existing technologies that might or might not have had their own working Basque terms at the time, such as "elevator." Pelot uses *berigan*, a term she invented—as far as I know—instead of the official term, *igogailu*. *Ber* might possibly be related to *behera* ("down"), while *igan* means "to elevate" in the northern Basque dialects. *Igogailu*, on the other hand, literally means "device to go up," which is what "elevator" means, of course. In those cases, I have gone for the accepted term in US English.

The second group encompasses all non-existent technology at the time of writing, such as *arroltzmatiko* (wheel-free, hovering individual vehicles), which I have translated as "ovamobile" (*arroltz* meaning "egg"); or *eskutel* (a small radio device that is worn on the wrist), which I have translated as "handphone" (*esku* meaning "hand"). In these cases, Pelot's neologisms have given me the chance to create my own in English.

And finally we have some very special examples of technology that already existed in the 1980s, in fields where the *lingua franca* was and is English—most notoriously computer science. In these cases, Pelot apparently decided to come up with Basque terms and concepts to replace the global English term. One renaming I really enjoyed was a computer button called *lot/buka*, which, after some head-banging, I figured could well refer to the on/off button. *Lotu* means to link, to connect, to tie up. *Bukatu*, on the other hand, means to end, to finish, kill, or break. While I could have gone for "on/off," which would have been accurate enough, I believed that it missed transmitting Pelot's way of thinking in her construction of language. Therefore, you will find it as "Link/Break" in the text.

Technology, however, is not the only thing with which Pelot had fun when it comes to pushing the limits of Basque. Short stories such as "Choppy Water" and "The Exchange" attest to the pleasure she took in the lyrical possibilities of her elliptical, synthetic style of writing.

As a reader who has been inspired all her life by translated books — which outside of the English-speaking world we simply call "books," to paraphrase an Italian colleague who made this point at an International Translation Day conference in the British Library years ago — I would not want to direct your eyes too much toward the nuts and bolts sustaining the stories and away from the stories themselves. May this note just add to your enjoyment of Mayi Pelot's science fiction, not distance you from it. I hope the work I have done will reach its ultimate goal to let you, readers, be absorbed and carried away by the stories.

Arrate Hidalgo, December 2, 2021

Miren

MIREN GOT HOME at 17:00. She was exhausted, but there was no time to lose. She stood at her front door and waited for the electronic eye to recognize her. The door opened quietly. After taking a carnation-scented bath, she chose a green robe and put it on. She combed her thick auburn hair for a long time and even put make-up on, carefully. She wanted to look distinguished and beautiful that evening.

She slowly re-read the durable message that was on her studio desk (a sheet of hyperwax; the other messages self-destructed if left outside their box for longer than five minutes). Then she put it in her bag. For a moment, Miren looked at Gorka's 3D portrait on the table.

The cameras at the doors of both her home and the elevator let her out onto the street, where the blue moving sidewalks took her to the station. Once there, she got into an ovamobile, a wheel-free vehicle that hovered 20 inches above the ground. Every main and side street had its own fleet of ovamobiles, which meant that people switching streets also needed to switch vehicles. Travel was covered by taxes, but all ovamobiles belonged to the Sigma society. Miren took off.

The building was ten miles away from the city. It was blue and spherical in shape.

The lobby had a purple hue. She entered the office to the left. There, a blue-haired android handed her the papers. It took her five minutes to fill out the file, thinking that they really didn't leave anything out in this place.

Afterwards, Miren made her way to the cafeteria. It was a space filled with white tables and seats that came in all sorts of shapes. The carpet muffled the sound of her footsteps; instead, she could hear a soft melody in the blue-lit air. Miren ordered a tea. She drank it calmly. It was delicious.

A while later, a pink android walked her to her room. There, the android set up the "mood-making" tape Miren had brought. The bed was propped against the wall to the right. It was legless, made of green viscose. Miren lay down. She was sleepy. She pressed a button.

Suddenly, the bedroom was replaced by a lush green mountain; on it stood a little cabin. Next to the cabin, a boy was playing txistu. She could see sheep, too. Miren closed her eyes.

Further out, by a river, a dog was frolicking. An eagle glided against the vivid blue sky.

Little by little, Miren's heart stopped.

The bedroom came silently back right away. The wall on the right opened, toppling the bed inside, in order to send the body out for incineration.

It was done as Miren had wished.

In the Entries office, the indicator for room number 11 lit up. The android fed the file into the carrier tube.

NAME Etxegorri, Miren 0600536779

MENTALLY HEALTHY yes no

CAUSE OF DEATH euthanasia

PERMISSION FOR EUTHANASIA ISSUED BY Dr Mello

REASON FOR EUTHANIZATION incurable illness

ILLNESS breast leprosy

CAUSE OF ILLNESS Patient worked on the coast, by the Anti-Pollution Wall

SEND NOTICE TO Lasa, Gorka 662236711

EUTHANIZATION requested before the due date in accordance with the law

THIS IS MY TRUE WISH 07/26/2040

Row, row

THAT MORNING, LITTLE Leyre saw the sea for the first time. She rushed into the V-school's long passageway and threw her cape into her little closet—it was a mystery how she hadn't destroyed it yet—hearing the doors of the small rooms slamming shut one after the other. She was *finally* going to see the sea!

Now, alone in her own tiny classroom, with her aurals on and the mic in front of her, she was staring at the teacher's 3D face.

"As we have seen, in the 20th century, our country was divided into two parts. Each was under French and Spanish rule. Nowadays, the entirety of Spain belongs to Iran, while Western Europe is part of the United States of the World. We're going to watch a film now. Pay attention! It's in 2D, so you might find it difficult to follow."

The teacher's face turned off with a click and, in its place, an old photograph appeared. Leyre thought it was too blue. A flat robotic voice said:

"This is the coast of the Bask Country in the 20th century. See the people lying on the sand." Click. "People swimming in the sea, like in today's swimming pools..." Click. "Here are a handful of boats in the open sea." Click, click, click.

Each student, in their individual rooms, stared at one picture after another, astonished by the unbelievable green color of the sea.

"This is a fountain. Back then, the water from many of those fountains was good for drinking. Nowadays, we do not waste water in this way: our cities purify their contaminated water and put them back to use. In 1995, the Atlantic Ocean was so contaminated that it was walled off. Some rivers were treated and redirected. The rest—that is, the ones that flow into the sea—have been buried." Click. "The ones you are looking at right now, Aturri and Errobia, run beneath our feet, in Byorn." Click. "Sigma society homes were built on top of them."

An old map of the Bask Country appeared on screen.

"In the countryside, which on this map is shown as the regions called Baxenabarre and Xiberoa, drinking from rivers has remained a practice until today. This is thanks to the Anti-Pollution Wall, of course. The Wall may block the sea from view, but it also protects us from it."

Some numbers began to appear and disappear on screen one by one. They said that in the countryside there was a 30% chance of contamination; on the coast, up to 3 miles from the Wall, the chance was 90%. In most cities of the United States of the World, there was a 50% chance of contamination. Leyre didn't understand.

"Therefore, the Wall is not enough. The Sigma society, always at your service, is preparing a big experiment in Byorn so that everybody can have a better life. Perhaps you, the youngest ones, will live again in a clean world. Now look at the sea today." Click.

Leyre choked back a scream. The water, from the horizon to the shore, was completely covered in waste, violently breaking in waves against the Wall. The little girl began to cry. Gazing at the oily black water of the open ocean, she remembered her late aunt's face, her father's words: *If she hadn't worked on the coast, she would still be with us.*

That morning, little Leyre saw the sea for the first time.

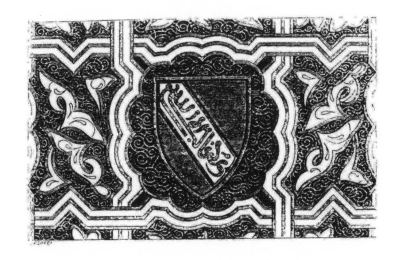

Feedback

CORDOBA WAS HOT under the spring sun. Were it not for the fact that the sidewalks moved, year 1417 in the old city could well look like the 20th century. (Hijri year 1417, that is; 2039 in the Christian calendar.) The streets were bustling with people walking here and there, some looking at their watches: there wasn't much time, but why rush? Allah would give them as long as they needed. Words, jokes, laughter, children's screaming floated in the air. The city's breath.

The clock hit fifteen hours. In the new neighborhood, in one of the buildings of the Sâd society, a 35-year-old man was lying on the floor. There was nobody else in the room. As the blinds fell delicately, like sleepy eyelids, a pleasant woman's voice began to guide him toward relaxation.

Lying there, Nizam tried to empty his mind. A break, at last! It made him happy to think of the well-earned 40 minutes of peace he had after five hours of work. His eyes were now free from all the craziness of the screens dancing about. They were empty. He forgot about his legs next. Like all societies of the world, here too Sâd had incorporated relaxation exercises into the daily schedules. Thanks to this method, that last sixth hour of work was an absolute pain.

"Be conscious of your left arm…your hand is resting on the ground…. It feels increasingly heavier…and heavy…er…" intoned the pleasant voice. Nizam's mind knew the exercise so well that it easily obeyed the voice. It actually knew the exercise too well, so Nizam couldn't push his worries aside.

Muslims get a 20-minute break; the rest of the world gets half an hour. There's no way I'll relax today.

And the 20 minutes passed, giving way to the next 20 of prayer. The pleasant sounds and voice quieted little by little. In the Mosque of Córdoba (which in Christian times was a Cathedral), the fourth program switched awake, halting the ovamobiles and the moving sidewalks. In Nizam's office, the blinds rolled up automatically, and a yellow arrow lit up in a corner over the wooden floor, indicating the direction of Mecca. Nizam sighed, walked towards the prayer rug placed under the arrow, and knelt down. The sound of a silver bell grew louder over the city—the recording of an ancient bell, now exhibited in a glass cabinet in Teheran.

Meanwhile, the protection robots activated and the electronic automuezzin began to sing the third prayer.

Then, all of Spain bowed at once.

It wasn't time for prayer in Tehran. Reza Ayatollah, President of Iran, was thinking. Bad news: the government of India, under Iranian power, had fallen. It was quite the blow for Iran. An unacceptable one. What's more, he could not forget about the Muslims of India and Pakistan—brothers must not kill brothers. What could he do? There were the micromissiles, he'd have to use them. But from where? Maybe he could just confiscate some other country's missiles and use those…

He'd need a new secret launching platform for that, Reza thought, as his hands hit the keyboard. He checked the time in Cordoba. It would have to wait.

In Cordoba, the automuezzin had gone silent. People were standing up, getting back into ovamobiles, walking on the—once again—moving sidewalks; the light arrows in homes, offices, and shops died. The Grand Ayatollah's 3D portrait appeared for a moment and soon disappeared again. Nizam was already standing, reading over his notes on the small screen of his typer.

"Peace be with you, brother!"

Nizam started, not having heard the door opening, and felt something darkening inside him as he replied to Sadegh with a "And with you, brother." *Peace,* he thought. But said nothing.

"Have you drawn up any conclusions?" Nizam asked.

"Well, in my opinion, anyway—"

Nizam stretched out his arm to stop Sadegh in his tracks.

"Allah gave us one tongue and two ears, brother, so that we listen twice before we speak. I've written up a summary of the documents I've been researching. This is what the telememory says: *In the 20th century, in the region we now call the Desert, there were four provinces belonging to the Bask Country: Nafarroa, Gipuzkoa, Bizkaia, and Araba. In the year 1370 (1992 AD), an unidentified accident took place in a Bizkaian nuclear power plant. The computer hasn't been able to give me any details. After that, the southern part of the Bask Country was officially declared a 'no-go zone.'*"

"That's impossible!" exclaimed Sadegh. "We know that no-go zones are one of the consequences of the Third World War."

"Well, this one, at least, is not. Access was forbidden in 1992, that we know for sure."

"And what's the reason listed? You haven't looked it up?"

"There's no point. The Third War happened, both we and the enemy entered Spain, and many documents were destroyed. We don't even know what happened in that nuclear plant. A small explosion? An experiment? It could have been anything. I would certainly like to know. These days Iranians are in control of the whole peninsula, but nobody ever ventures into the desert any more. Not even on a small plane. Some hypotheses claim that the entire population died a long time ago; others say that there are still people living there. What could they be like? According to the telememory, the ones who did go there to find out never came back. What do you think? It's probably just a dead land. Nothing more."

"Let's at least try. We can send some androids."

"That we can do."

It was ten minutes to eighteen, almost time for the fourth prayer. Nizam had already washed his head and hands. The water hadn't helped with the headache. His head was throbbing with the words he didn't dare say out loud. He spoke to himself, trying to calm down.

Yes, we have built a great nation. All Muslims under the same flag: a crescent moon, decorated with nine stars. It's true. We must refuse the blind capitalism and inequality of non-Muslim countries. We live in Allah's equality and brotherhood, at least for now. Christian faith is waning, ours grows day by day, thanks to the new thinkers who helped reform Islam. And now, what? Instead of our technologist ayatollahs of the past, we have this one who is trying to wage holy war with micromissiles. Some wise man! He is not serving Allah, just himself—

The arrow lit up on the wood: it was time for fourth prayer.

In Teheran, Reza Ayatollah was mustering his patience. He pressed the **Link/Break** button to enter his password and then pressed **1**. As the Quran's index appeared on the small screen, Reza heard a weak clicking noise: the printer was working.

He pulled the sheet from the machine and read the message on it:

CAN'T BUILD MICROMISSILE LAUNCHING PLATFORM IN DESERT
NO NEWS FROM ANDROIDS DISPATCHED
NIZAM

Reza put the paper on the table and sat looking at it. He watched it as it burned without fire or smoke, turning to dust and floating away.

The Digital Maze

ANAIZ'S BED TURNED on at dawn. Week 19 had begun in New York. As the room lit up, a pleasant voice said "Good morning. It is day 1 of week 19, 2050. Good morning. It is day 1 of week 19, 2050..." repeatedly until Anaiz got up. Then, the voice said "Sigma wishes you a pleasant day" and fell silent, as the blind slid up noiselessly and the artificial lighting went off.

It was becoming brighter outside. Down on the street, the passageways connecting the buildings blocked every last corner of the sky from view. There were no squares. No trees. The entire city was just street after street. It wasn't so gloomy—the buildings boasted every color and shape. If you looked down at them from a plane, you would see the group of streets and building roofs forming the shape of the Greek letter sigma, a great Σ, on the ground. There was the Temple of the Mind, Sigma Corp's large labs and offices. It was also where the main computers of the United States of the World and the dwellings of some Sigmans were located. Anaiz Etxeberry lived there.

That first morning of the week, the young woman went to the kitchen and turned on the wallscreen before settling down to breakfast. No surprises in the morning news: a group of Panslavian aircrafts had been spotted in Indian airspace. The president of the USW would not tolerate any more Iranians near Perpignan. The usual shenanigans, in sum. A different machine was installed on each of the kitchen's green walls. On the longest wall, across from the door, was the meal dispenser with its small lights and buttons on the right-hand side and, on the other, a little transparent door that resembled that of an oven. The door opened automatically and produced hot foods on metallic trays. Over on the right there was a small keyboard with which one could choose and program the week's menu. On the left-hand wall was the drink dispenser, with its own keyboard and compartments. Each key had the name of a drink on it; the machine could even put sugar in. The automatic hyper-ice box was by the door.

Anaiz pressed **Button 3**, and out of the compartment came a hot café latte in a paper cup. Everything being built into the walls, the room had no furniture except for a table and a single chair. Anaiz pressed a button on the table, and the board opened up, revealing a metal tray containing buttered toast rising up from the middle. Even though the apartment had been renewed, or so Anaiz thought, it had a classic-style living room: you had to bring the food and drinks from the kitchen yourself.

Anaiz felt satisfied with the comfortable life that the job she had found in New York afforded her, but she found the absence of sky disturbing. She had been born in Europe, the old continent that had been bled out by World War Three, and she wouldn't have been able to lead such a life in her hometown. In her father's house (as everywhere else in the Bask Country), food was still stored inside furniture, instead of in the walls, and they cooked it in pots and pans. If she were in the Bask Country—but enough with the self-pity. "Anyway, at least I was lucky to find a position at the Sigma society as an archigrapher. Who knows, they might give me work in Byorn at some point."

As she walked past the living room, she looked at the printer in the small media room: no messages. She headed to work in high spirits.

WORK BACK HOME

MR. NATANAEL OPUSDAY, director—officially, "coordinator"—of the Sigma Society, was typing at his computer, searching for Basks among his workforce. The answer was positive: 50 people. *How many in Byorn?*, he typed. "20." *In what venues?* "Automatic kitchens, hotels, hospitals, pharmaceutical labs." (Too specialized, these last ones.) Natanael Opusday didn't need anyone like that. He typed in his preference for schedulers or archigraphers, secretarial types. Affirmative. There was one. Anaiz Etxeberry. 00.2027.30.15.1524.

▲

In workcube number 144, Anaiz let out a sigh. She had summarized and organized the notes she had typed up during that morning's conference and written up schedule ΣEH 2050-0205. She could see it all on the terminal's screen. Finally, her fingers left the keyboard. She had to re-read the text before pressing the **Send** button. There were no errors — wait, yes: two spelling mistakes. No big deal; the telewriter would take care of those.

▲

Mr. Opusday had been shocked by the low numbers of Bask workers in the Sigma Society. Why, though? He decided he needed to call on the psychomemory before going to that Etxeberry. The computer filled him in: after World War Three, there was a scarcity of both people and food throughout Europe. Most Basks had undertaken agriculture and stockbreeding with Agriglobal financial aid and were now growing rich thanks to selling foodstuffs to the new Sigma offices in the area, according to the statisticians' reports.

"We're off to a great start, it seems," Nathanael thought bitterly to himself. He kept reading: "People tied to the soil. Could be the old-fashioned type. They're not, though — they do use the Sigma terminals we installed in every town. And have new methods to work the land. Do they live scattered in country houses? Ah, no, they have agritowns. Wow, and there's even an underground nuclear shelter in each one! The War taught these people that fear of the bomb was basic common sense."

As soon as Anaiz pressed the **Send** button, the little red light on her desk started blinking: a call from the director. She pushed the green **Audiovisual** button, after which the lights went off in her workcube to reveal the boss's office. Anaiz was shocked to see Natanael Opusday himself in front of her. *The boss, giving* me *a call?*

▲

Opusday's look wasn't the cold, hard stare she had anticipated. In fact, those black eyes calmly looking at Anaiz's cubicle didn't transmit anything in particular to her. As soon as he appeared, he took everything in; the confidential Kyklops files were right:

Anaiz was a good employee, judging by the fact that all there was on her desk was a lined notepad and an old pencil. Everybody typed in the 21st century, but psychostatisticians had proven that clerks needed to have toys, trinkets, and such on their desks, as people listened more attentively when doodling or manipulating something with their hands. That is why all Sigma workers were granted the right to decorate their offices. Most of them chose a notepad and pencil, probably nostalgic for their school days. All children learned how to write by hand. What would they do, after all, if another war put all machines down? Opusday smiled to himself. *Not* all *of them...*

Anaiz's voice brought her boss back from his thoughts. "Co-ordinator, sir...I sent out a summary of the morning conference a minute ago."

"Never mind that," interrupted Opusday. Ah, yes. According to the file, Anaiz was E.A.S., an emotional type. He'd have to go easy on her. "Don't be scared! You're going back to your home country. That's right: you'll be working in the new Byorn office, located in the nearby Hazparn area. You leave tomorrow morning. Jep Weber, an engineer, will fill you in. You are to start work on 19-4. Until then you might want to accompany a group of tourists who are in the area, but that's up to you, okay? You'll find the references in your media room."

The boss's image disappeared. Anaiz was ecstatic. At long last! She'd get to work back home!

By 17:00 her suitcase was stuffed and closed. Anaiz pulled a hyperwax message from the media room printer. The green sheet contained only a few words: "Weber, Jep. Engineer. 01.2025.18.03.534. Meet at Hazparn office." Sigmans sure didn't waste time.

When Anaiz gave her father the good news on the video-phone, the poor man could hardly believe it. "My daughter, assigned for the new Byorn office at 23!" It was in the Bask Country where experts and technologists from the USW and Panslavia celebrated their conferences, which meant that not everybody could gain access to those offices. The "tourists" worked there.

Most of the time, foreigners spent a week there, working up to the weekend. When a debate or any unexpected problems arose, they worked nights too, taking meal and relaxation breaks set up by a sociopsychologist. But the weekends were sacred, and locals "accompanied" and prepared holiday plans for those who wished. At this point, Basks called those two days "tourists in" and "tourists out." Local farmers sold food to hotels, a few of which belonged to people from the town. The rest belonged to Sigma. "I'm glad that Sigma is growing," Anaiz's father had said. "It brings money in. Did you know that Sigma's buying more and more from us? And we're receiving more support from the government. You're coming back at a great time."

"So you must be getting more visitors, then?"

Her father's face darkened a little.

"Actually, no…. There are about as many people as usual. Maybe, I don't know."

▲

It was 8 in the morning, and Anaiz was on the plane to Byorn, remembering her father's words. The Government and Sigma, buying huge quantities of food…. Why? People didn't go hungry in the USW. Ersatz food was a thing of the past. What were they stocking up for? Maybe they were planning on expanding Byorn.

She went straight to Hazparn without seeing her parents. She found a terminal in the Sigma building's great lobby. Anaiz typed in the code 383614; the **Link/Break** button signaled that Kyklops, the program to locate people, was ready to respond.

| PERSON | PRESS [1] | THEN SEND |
| PLACE | PRESS [2] | THEN SEND |

Anaiz input Weber's reference.

A list came up:

two Webers, Jep and John. Brothers, perhaps.

Each had his own videophone number, linked to different workcubes. She exited Kyklops and sent a videocall to Weber's workbox. In vain. She didn't leave a message; it would be better

21

to just look for him. "I'll have plenty of time to use the answering machine if I can't find him." She started Kyklops again, pressed **2** and then **Send**, and began to check the common spaces. She looked in the hotel; nothing. The hospital? No Weber. In the end, a pretty red-haired secretary at the ovamobile station told her that Weber hadn't "returned from the crash course yet." That surprised Anaiz. A crash course stretching on more than expected? She'd thought that sort of thing never happened to Sigmans.

"Probably good old Weber met a pretty Panslav there," said the secretary, and then cut the conversation short, as if she thought she had already talked too much. It was obvious to Anaiz that the woman was jealous. And lying. People attending courses always had the weekends free precisely for that sort of thing. Anaiz had a strange thought: If somebody had done that Weber in, this would be quite the crime novel, and she'd be right in the middle of it. The Interkyklops put an end to the hypothetical crime soon enough. The course in Zakopane (on planning skills for communities) had indeed been extended until 19-5. Jep Weber was there. With the mystery out the window, Anaiz called on Kyklops a third time to find out where her workcube was. She looked at the floor plan that appeared on the screen: a blinking red dot indicated cubicle number **25**. She headed there, and, once she had sent a message to Weber's workcube, she took an ovamobile to her parents' house. On the way, she mentally gathered what she had learned about the man: *Okay, so the secretary has called him "good old Weber," so either they're close or he's a bit of a player. In any case, I'm a newcomer, so I'll have to be nice to everyone.*

▲

The videophone's call grew louder in the old house's wood-furnished living room, in Ortzaize. The Etxeberrys stood in line in front of the kitchen block; they were preparing lunch. The father was placing the meat in the automatic burner, the mother was getting the flatware out of the dishwasher, and Anaiz was having fun attempting to make chapatis on an old pancake pan. Her father turned on the burner, initiated the program, and soon returned from taking the call, saying "It's for Anaiz. Weber." Then he deftly grabbed the pan from his daughter's hands. Anaiz didn't mind. She knew her father was a good cook.

On the media room's screen, she saw nothing but somebody's darkened back, from which came the words "Sorry, please hold just one second." Then Weber appeared with a cheerful smile, and Anaiz, looking more carefully past him, recognized the reddish light and plastic palm trees of the Horsemen's swimming pool. She realized he had a beautiful body. *Good old Weber seems one to enjoy earthly pleasures. Time will tell.*

"Good morning, Mr Weber."

"Call me Jep."

"Jep, I've been told I need you in order to get started with my work."

Jep smiled at her.

"No, Anaiz. It's actually me who needs you: you're a local and me, I just got here. And I'm totally out of step, to boot! After spending an entire month in Panslavia..."

A month-long crash course?

"Where?" asked Anaiz, and immediately thought it was a dumb question. She already knew. Or maybe not, not really. And, in any case, it was better to play dumb with this sort of men.

"Zakopane, in the country known as Poland."

"What were you doing there?"

Weber huffed, ran a hand through his blond hair.

"Studying group planning. You know the Sigma principles: everybody has their own job, but sometimes one has to do something else, and so on. I just...don't know much about the Bask Country. I've brought a bunch of Panslavs with me. I'll be with them at the Byorn fronton, at 5. Come with us."

This guy was clearly living the good life: young, well built, cheerful...

"All right, until 5, then. Thank you —"

"Bye."

▲

At 5, Weber and the Panslavs were relaxing in the fronton. A pelota game was on. It was terrific. Robot pelota players and dancers, well organized. Weber was transfixed. When the ball went off court, as a force field bounced it back inside with a weird sound, Weber looked at Anaiz instead.

"Is it true that people still dance in the countryside, Anaiz?" he asked.

"It is."

"And they play pelota as well?"

"Also true."

"But androids are a better choice for tourists. They never miss, they're always on time, don't get drunk or angry…or paid," said Weber, grinning.

Anaiz, Weber, and the Panslavs delved into the customary small-talk.

"Anaiz, how can the language of such a small people have survived?"

"The Bask Country was isolated for a long time after World War Three," Anaiz explained. "French almost disappeared in France, which was razed by the war, except in the Lyon area. If French has survived to this day, it is thanks to Helvetia, Quebec, and Belgium, that country the 20th century French were constantly making fun of. Meanwhile, Bask increasingly took over mass media and got into all of the schools. The Bask Country has been through great poverty, just like the rest of Western Europe. Even now, the rural areas are quite poor, technologically speaking. Byorn is the only city in the Bask Country, and if it's automated, that's thanks to Sigma."

▲

That weekend in the Arbona conservatory, among the blue plastic palm trees, was a beautiful time to enjoy being naked under the real sun.

"Anaiz?"

"Jep?"

"Do you know why Sigma has brought you here?" he asked.

"I don't?"

"Because you're both an archigrapher and a Bask speaker. That means you can give technical presentations in Bask," Jep explained.

"So I won't be doing my job anymore?"

"Nope. You'll be doing PR. Hey, sorry! Look at me, talking shop on a weekend! Come on, we'll get sunburnt if we stay out like this much longer. And it's been three weeks since I last went for a swim. I can feel my head swelling. Three, two, one, go!"

And Weber left Anaiz alone on the sand, rushed with a little dance to the swimming pool, dived in tumbling, and splashed back up with a smile on his face.

THE WALL AND THE DOME

"AS YOU CAN see, despite the tremendous work being done by the robots on the seaside, coastal contamination spreads day by day. This is the Anti-Pollution Wall, with its overlook..."

The holofilm showed the Wall while Anaiz's voice provided the commentary. In Luhuso's meeting V-hall, the locals watched the holofilm that Anaiz had recorded. She was standing amidst the Luhuso townspeople, waiting for their comments. She remembered the overlook. She had seen the inner side of the Wall from the conservatories many times, but had never gone up to the top of the Wall itself, where the overlook was located, until Weber had brought her there. There she had learned about her new job.

She remembered the red ovamobile halting by the moving sidewalk with its distinctive sound. She and Jep had walked from the sidewalk to the footbridge. Treading the inner edge of the Wall, Anaiz admired the polychromatic statues, the tide, the whirlpools, the shimmering waves dancing endlessly, making her dizzy.

"Anaiz, pay attention! Come out here."

Weber and Anaiz had placed their official permissions (a hyperwax band) on the intercoms; the doors had closed silently behind them. Anaiz was tired, but the oxygen from her mask quickly woke her up. Weber had begun telling her the details:

"These walls against coastal contamination are most probably impossible to crack."

"Most probably?" started Anaiz.

"To this day, nothing like that has happened around here. Anyway, the robots here keep watch on both the Wall and the sea, day and night."

The elevator had taken them to the great lounge where the overlook had been built. Various machines filled the space. The walls were made of Plexiglas. Each robot was busy at its own workbench. Standing, of course; robots didn't need to sit. They were metallic and mute.

"There are no androids?" Anaiz had asked.

"They're no good for this, Anaiz. Robots are cheaper and faster. But they did paint them in the country's colors, to make them more aesthetically pleasing. The red ones look at the sea—well, they analyze it, to be exact. The green ones work at the Wall."

The robots' red eyes were constantly turning and moving. They did have eyes, but no face, which made for a disturbing effect.

Anaiz had seen the murky, oily sea waves through the transparent walls. It was sickening. But she wanted to know.

"Jep, let's go outside."

"We can't. Humans are forbidden from going outside, even with masks. The Wall is solid for now, good enough to keep the country's groundwater clean, but it won't be for long. That's why the Sigma society has developed a new method. We've discovered a new material that's extra hard, transparent, soundproof, and indestructible."

"What's it called?"

"Hyperglass," Jep had said.

"And this new material is being used to build another wall?"

Weber had let out a sigh. It must have been a stupid thing to say, Anaiz thought.

"That's why you've been brought over here. Walls aren't enough. There'll be an experiment in Byorn: the city will be covered up."

"Covered up?"

"Yes, by a hyperglass dome. The city will become a shelter against contamination from the coast."

"So the rural areas will be left out of the dome, then. That's not right."

"Another one will be made later on. It'll be raised and secured with force fields."

"And what do you need me for in all this?" Anaiz had asked.

"The force field generators need to be placed on the outskirts. You'll reach out to the people who own those lands and explain everything to them. You'll have to record a holofilm and show them that too. In Bask, of course. Also, people will feel like they can talk to someone born and bred in their country. You'll take care of the contracts, trying to make them sell to Sigma the lands where the machines will go."

▲

Anaiz kept thinking about that conversation. Since then, she had been traveling from town to town, giving the same talk and playing the same holofilm.

A cough (or was it a comment?) pulled her from her thoughts. Anaiz remembered that she was standing in the middle of the Luhuso meeting V-hall. The holofilm was repeating the same figures that children learned at V-school:

> "Chance of contamination in the rural areas: 30%
> On the coast, up to 3 miles from the Wall: 90%
> In most USW cities: 50%
> The wind carries harmful substances from the seaside..."

How many times had she played this film? She had been talking to a lot of farmers. At first, people didn't trust her. Then, after they saw the images of the cracks in the Wall and the illnesses suffered by seaside workers (especially breast leprosy) in the holofilm, most people got scared and agreed to the dome's construction, signing contracts with Sigma. Yes, how many times now had she seen people shift from mistrust to fear. Talk, questions, holofilm, people got scared, contracts were signed; talk, questions, holofilm, people got scared, contracts were signed…. Anaiz's life had become a broken record. A record that would need turning over at some point: on the other side, a city, and later, an entire country sheltered under the dome. Imprisoned under the dome.

However, that day, perhaps because she was already bored with the holofilm, doubt rose in Anaiz's mind. A 90% contamination risk by the sea, 30% in the rural areas…meaning, not much. But Weber said the Wall was still in good condition. And there weren't that many breast leprosy cases in Byorn. *Are the coast and the seaside the same thing? The countryside gets wind from the toxic south, too!*

That afternoon she confessed her doubts to Weber. He insisted that the dome was just an experiment, something they were building "just in case." She knew how public relations were about adorning the truth a little, didn't she?

"I understand that, Jep, but—"

"You must be so *tired*," he cut her off. "Let's go dancing, or swimming!"

Finally, Anaiz resorted to searching for the figures herself in her workcube. She turned on the terminal, indicated the beginning of the message with the **Link/Break** button, typed in the words "coastal contamination," and pressed the **Send** button. She read the index on the topic that appeared on screen:

COASTAL CONTAMINATION ■
1. LIST AND HISTORY OF CONTAMINATED TOWNS
2. MAPS AND STATISTICS
3. …

She waited for the screen to load completely, not bothering to look at item number 3, and chose number 2. There it was. The figures that the database gave her were lower than the ones in the holofilm. The maps also proved that the contamination on the coast was lower than she thought. Had somebody got it wrong? And if not, why had they changed the numbers? Without a second thought, Anaiz pressed **Correct**. Nothing happened except for a line of text on the screen:

TO RETRIEVE MORE DETAILS
RETURN TO INDEX

Suddenly she heard a ring. She remembered that the offices were closing for the day, and all posts had to be vacated within ten minutes. She thought it would be best to shut down the terminal, and videophone Weber from home.

So she did. Weber's mocking answer was "What? So the holofilm numbers are inflated. Look at me caring! You really must be so worn out. Have you already forgotten what PR is all about? How are we supposed to convince people with a bunch of sad tiny numbers?" Jep stopped talking, looked her in the face, and, softening his eyes and tone, continued: "Anaiz, let's go out this afternoon, yeah? Meet you at the Brindos swimming pool, around 17:30, okay? Can we do this? And please, forget about work! A girl as pretty as you, doing research aside from all the work she already has to do. It's not important. If you ever come to me again with this kind of stuff, I'll strangle you with these hands," Jep said, shaking his tan hands with an irritated grin. "See you later, then?"

"All right."

Weber's image faded out.

▲

The water was purple in the Brindos swimming pool; the fake sun, with its own thermostat, cast a reddish light. The newest music hits hovered in the air. There was no sand: the ground was covered in a bluish-green substance, smoother than silk cloth. Every now and then, soft flashes on the reddish walls blinked in time with parts of the songs. Anaiz and Weber fell to the ground, out of breath. They were back from the psychodance hall above, where they had got into an "action-game" — or creativity exercise — with another two coworkers, making up the most delirious moves and dancing to the music that came from the sound machine. It was a really nice group.

"Hi, Anaiz! It's been ages! How's life treating you?"

Anaiz looked up. She recognized two young friends of hers.

"Baldi…Kepa. This is Jep. I'm a Sigman now, and I'll be working here at home from now on."

The three men began to talk. Kepa and Baldi soon revealed what Anaiz had not mentioned: they were farmers and sons of farmers. Baldi at least did farming full-time. It was a whole new world to Weber. He wanted to know everything there was to know about the Bask Country.

"What kind of relationship do you have with Spain?" he asked.

Kepa, Baldi, and Anaiz looked at one another. Finally, it was Baldi who spoke:

"There's no relationship."

"Why? Is it because Spain belongs to Iran?"

"No, it's because of the Desert that separates the Bask Country from Spain. It's a no-go zone. It used to be a part of our country."

"Ah, yes. I heard something about that. But there can't still be radioactivity around there at this point, can there? It's forbidden to go in there, right? And you've had no news since?"

"Just stories." Kepa took over. "Stuff like the fish in the sea over there has changed a lot, or people themselves turning into fish, or half fish. Monsters inland…" He sighed. "Anyway, Iran has other problems to worry about, now that the Indian government has fallen, apparently."

"And what's all this about a dome?" Baldi suddenly asked.

That startled Weber.

"What? You haven't watched the holofilm? Our very own Anaiz's magnum opus? Unforgivable!"

"We've watched it, all right. But since we have a Sigman right here, why not interview you a little about i—?"

Weber interrupted Baldi with a groan.

"Have you all set out to kill me? Not even a minute's rest. And besides, you've learned most everything there is to know already, the rest is all very technical details, you know." He huffed. "My head's about to burst! And my throat's dry. Who wants a drink?"

▲

On day 3 of week 24, Anaiz woke up to find her father hurrying toward her.

"Anaiz! You've got a message on the printer. Read it! It says you've got to go to the office."

YOU CAN'T GIVE ANY TALKS TODAY. COME INTO THE OFFICE. WE NEED TO TRACE A DETAILED PLAN FOR THE DOME. SOMEONE FROM THE RECORDS OFFICE IS SUPPOSED TO CREATE A MEMODISK FOR SAID DOME.

SENT BY SIGMA

As Anaiz walked into her workcube, she saw a page of hyperwax coming out of the printer: references to maps of towns in the region. The machine was far too bright for Anaiz—after partying with Weber, she had gone to sleep late and was still half asleep. The message's words began to go round and round in her head. "Dome," "create memodisk," "memodisk for said dome".... That is the reason why, as soon as she connected the terminal, her fingers unconsciously typed in the word "dome."

Anaiz, you dummy! she thought. And then she remembered she had the reference for that item. *Perhaps.... Let's find out what it looks like.* And she pressed **Send**. The computer brought up an index:

DOME ❏
Index ❏
1. What is the dome
2. Architecture
3. Styles and classes
4. The New Byorn mission

None of the first three had anything to do with Byorn, so she pressed **4** as she repeated the words she had never heard together before: *New Byorn—could it be? A refurbished Byorn?*

The screen went yellow: the S0 signal. In order to disclose item 4, she had to dial Sigma's private computer. Anaiz immediately entered the S0 code: 10000010. Astonished, she found a record of her own notes (the plan to install the machines to hold up the dome, the list of farmers who had accepted, and so on) and even a reference to her holofilm.

"Anaiz, what are you doing?" shouted Weber, storming into the room, rushing to the keyboard and brusquely pressing **Cancel.** "It can't be! What were you thinking of, you silly girl? Everybody else is getting hell trying to keep up with work on the dome, and here you are, wasting time! Do you think we have time for this nonsense?"

Despite the anger she felt, Anaiz replied to him as calmly as she could manage: "When have I wasted time? I have always finished my work well ahead of schedule, both here and in New York. I don't know what you're so riled up about."

Weber bit his lip. "Forgive me. I'm a little tired, and..." He gave her a fake smile. "But that doesn't mean I regret last night." With a little sigh, he slowly placed his hand on Anaiz's shoulder, not looking at her. "Well, we have a lot of work to do on the dome, and we have to do it soon. And in any case, you don't have to dial the database; you've been long aware of all the details. You won't find out much new. There's no point. Now, back to work! Gotta go. See you later."

The man tilted his head, then added:

"You forgive me, don't you, babe?"

"Sure, Jep."

Weber left the room smiling. But it was obvious that he would be watching her every move. Anaiz was completely on edge. *Yesterday I was in his arms, today he's attacking me with nonsense. Maybe I'm being too tough on him. He's tired because of me, because he went home late. But even so, after the way he talked to me, at least he could've kissed me on his way out.... Hey, enough of this! I'd better get to work.*

Anaiz would have forgotten all about it, except Jep came noiselessly back an hour later. The woman, feeling a presence at her back, turned her head. Weber was peeking over her shoulder at the terminal screen. Then he understood Anaiz had seen him and, smiling affectionately, waved at her and left without stepping in. If he was in such a rush, what had he come for? Mistrust awoke in Anaiz.

If he's to watch me like this, he won't be able to do anything else. And what is he lurking around me for, anyway? Does he like me that much? He hasn't said he loves me or anything like that, and now he's acting like he's jealous or something. No, it's not jealousy. It's something else.

Anaiz took the telestylus from the table and used it on the screen, creating a bright blue line. She could think while she doodled.

He says he has a lot of work to do, but every time I ask him for details, he plays dumb. Once he said he wanted to dance, another time he said we weren't at work. So why does he now come creeping up behind me, like some thief? He doesn't want me dialing the database. Why? I've never missed a deadline. So what is it? He thinks I'm just a mindless, diligent worker he can keep out of the loop, and nothing more!

Out of the loop...Anaiz felt the realization hitting her like a hammer. So Weber did know what was going on. Something she was not supposed to know. Could it be related to the database somehow? He had gotten so angry when he saw her reading about the dome. What could it be?

"Hey, what am I doing?" Anaiz said to herself. The telestylus had dropped from her hand, leaving a crooked line on the screen. She began to correct the drawing with the **Remove** button. *Two different sets of figures about the dome available, and one is false. Weber seems to accept that, keeps saying it doesn't matter. And then he keeps watch on me! It must be more important than he's saying.*

The videophone made a ping. It was Weber.

"Would having dinner together this evening be enough to show you I'm sorry?"

Jep was acting all innocent again.

"Sure, Jep. See you soon!" Anaiz said, and hung up wondering what the real purpose of that dome could be.

⚓

By week 28, "New Byorn" was covered by a transparent dome. Natanael Opusday, director of the Sigma society, sat in his new office looking at the first photograph of the city. For a long time. He was happy: a job well done. He heard a weak ping and turned off the photograph, which instantly revealed the room again. Best to keep the picture out of sight. He said "Yes, come in" on the intercom. The visitor appeared at once, and the door closed silently behind him.

They spent an hour talking. At some point, Opusday decided that replying to this visitor's questions was a waste of his time. He sighed at him.

"Look, Mr. Lasa. There is no need for this to turn into an argument. What's the point?"

Gorka Lasa's eyes were fixed on the fat man in his thirties in front of him. Opusday continued: "I understand your concerns. The union has sent you to let us know about your problems, that's normal. But how many workers are we actually going to leave out of work? Just a few."

"Yeah, sure. A few, except for every single worker in town, of course!"

"Please, listen to me. Sigma took those workers in to build the dome. No questions asked! They all knew that the dome's construction wouldn't last forever. They knew it was temporary. Besides, after that work, we have even offered them new jobs. We're about to set up a project on planet Mars. Some are already working there."

"What about those who have always lived in Byorn? How many of them have left, unable to face the rising costs of living there? Have you offered jobs to them, too?"

"You don't have any workers.... I mean, you have no Sigma members to hire. It's not our problem if living prices have gone up, that's the market. It's not our fault, and we have nothing to do with it. And yet, we'll be doing everything we can—"

Gorka interrupted him.

"What about that new tax? That one that everybody who lives in Byorn except for Sigmans has to pay? You have nothing to do with that either, I presume!"

Natanael Opusday sighed again.

"You won't understand me. It's hard to believe, but it's the truth: that decision was made by the government. Sigma didn't ask for it. We have our own problems, too. Don't forget that Sigma isn't like other societies—we are an experimental collective. We carry out experiments, it's what we do, and now we have to do it as soon as possible. That's why the government is helping…well, having us in mind. Maybe once the second dome covers the entire country you will realize the kind of headaches we've had to deal with."

At that point, Gorka thought he had already done his duty. Deep down, he knew it was too late.

"Is there anything else you would like to say now, Mr. Opusday?"

"Since the unemployment rate has gone up in these parts, we'll make an effort to offer some positions in South America. But what will the workers over there think of that?"

▲

Anaiz returned to her usual duties: this time, planning for the new sports center in New Byorn. She was happy, she didn't want to go back to New York. She was worried, too. She didn't want to see Weber on the weekend. She videophoned him with an excuse, said she wanted to see her parents. Weber didn't ask her any questions. Did he want to put some distance between them, too? Perhaps he did.

And so, on tourists out Sunday, Kepa, Anaiz, and Baldi were lying on their backs on a green hill. Lying down, but not asleep. Below they could see Gorka's red and white farmhouse. The three were friends, young, and Bask. The three were quiet—and in disagreement. Because Anaiz worked for Sigma. Because she had shown people the holofilm about the coast's contamination; she had made deals with them. Her young friends talked to her, and she felt it was as if they spoke from behind a wall made of glass, or hyperglass, finally to be silent again.

Anaiz gave up. She thought she could have come to the countryside for a break, to have fun and forget about her worries and doubts. The force field generators were already installed in the rural folks' lands. But even though the work was done, there was no peace for her. Everybody was bombarding her with questions she had heard millions of times by now: is the dome's hyperglass tough enough, can it be blown up, etc. At first Anaiz had thought that the experiment was worth it. She also thought that erecting the dome would be good for the country's economy. After all, the post-war baby boom and the machinery Sigma had brought to the country meant that some people had been forced to migrate, but young people had found work in the country thanks to the dome. Now, however, she didn't know what to think any more.

Baldi was singing an old song under his breath.

The sun kisses
our beautiful house…

Gorka's voice pulled her out of her ruminations. He had walked up the hill to where the three friends lay.

"One in two, Anaiz! Are you listening to me? One in two people have left Byorn in the past month. Some kicked out by Sigma according to the law, or so they say! Others have left for Mars because life in New Byorn has become too expensive for them. Soon there won't be a single local left, so you'll be able to declare Byorn squeaky clean; with the city under the dome, now all the filth is out: the coast contamination and us folk! Oh, yes. I know: us folk except for the Sigmans among us, don't worry. Hurray for Sigma. Long live Sigma. It was clear as day that your beloved monopoly wanted to throw us out, and now they have finally done it!"

Anaiz was angry.

"What do you mean *my* beloved Sigma? Just because I work for them? Other Basks do, too!"

"Yeah, sure, *the happy few*![1] New Byorn is for Sigma people. Sigma City! That's what you tricked us for, with all those false documents and all that hypocrisy. Run to your dear coworkers!"

Baldi, at last, opened his mouth. He and Anaiz had been close friends since they were very little.

"You're being too hard on her, but at the end of the day, you're right."

The remark made Anaiz want to run away. She stood up abruptly.

"Yeah. You're both right," Anaiz said. With difficulty she managed to say goodbye before running home, her words caught in her throat, and half crying.

▲

She got there as the final notes of the country's anthem played in the kitchen: Aida's trumpets. She pushed open the old door that led to the living room, where the wallscreen took her into the armored-wall clad office of the president of the USW. President Sam Nottobe, a sad look in his eyes, smiled prudently.

Anaiz listened intently.

"...especially after the terrible events unfolded in India, I am pleased to communicate a piece of good news: tomorrow I will attend peace negotiations from New Byorn, during my visit to its experimental shelter. Congratulations, Sigma members, for you are the ones battling the world's one and true enemy: coastal contamination. My dear citizens, this is all for now. Goodbye, everyone."

As soon as the wallscreen switched off, her father looked at her. The president's office had disappeared, bringing the old living room back, and with it, Anaiz's face.

"In other words," her father said, "this is going to become a big old international mess. Hey, what's wrong?"

Anaiz was crying.

"Is it because a group of Iranians have gone into India, or because they're lost? What do you expect, with that Ayatollah poking his nose into everything? Not even our president is as worried

---

1   In English in the original.

as you are, if he's leaving New York and coming all the way here to inaugurate the New Byorn dome. What's wrong? You're white as a ghost!"

"N-nothing, dad…. Gorka had a go at me."

"Gorka has goes at everybody. Since he lost his fiancée to breast leprosy, he can get very bitter. There's the union thing, as well. Don't pay him any mind."

"I'm going back to Byorn in the afternoon."

"So soon? But you're very tired."

"I know. I just have to get some work ready as soon as possible. But I'll come back and rest here. I'm not ill, dad. Don't worry."

"Need Weber to comfort you, eh? No, no, say no more," Anaiz's father said, cheerfully.

Fortunately, Anaiz said no more.

▲

"Mom, I want to see the sky!"

Little John had marveled at the clouds he could see from the plane that had brought him to New Byorn. Now, from its streets, the sky was invisible, and so was the dome. His mother was in a hurry. The blue moving sidewalks looked like rivers. It was pretty, but not that special. Mrs. Smith was impatient to see her new living quarters.

"Mom, where is the dome?"

"Up there, over the buildings, honey."

"Look, mom! What's that? Spiders!"

New Byorn was celebrating. The city fully deserved the "New" in its name. No single old house was left; all streets were now covered up and full of holographic images floating over them. On the street mother and son were walking on, the images were golden spiders, plucking pleasant sounds out of their webs, which were actually made of memory fiber. Suddenly, Mrs. Smith noticed a blue glass building and walked off of the moving sidewalk. With some difficulty, the boy read the name on it.

"Ger…ni…ka. Mom, what does it mean?"

"Don't know, sweetheart. Probably a flower's name, something like that."

The green door slid silently, and they went into the building, down a corridor, and into the elevator. As Mrs. Smith said "Here we are," a red glass door slid open, the light in the entrance turned on, and a choir of soft robot voices began to sing "Happy Birthday." The apartment was Mrs. Smith's birthday present. When the Government decree threw out non-Sigma members by declaring the entire city "an experiment site," many experts and technologists bought homes in the city at cheap prices. Later, Sigma sold apartments to some non-Sigma industrialists, as well. Among them, Mr. Smith.

Inside the apartment, Mrs. Smith was assessing it all. "It's small, but impeccably organized," her husband had said. The entrance had two doors; one led to the automatic kitchen, the other, to the living room. There were no other walls.

The living room consisted of three hyperglass "boxes": the bedroom, its ensuite bathroom, and on the right, the dining room, with its automatic dining table, directly linked to the appliances in the kitchen. The table was the only piece of furniture. The floor, walls, and ceiling were covered in viscose. A few bumps lined the floor: they transformed into chairs when one sat on them. The wall, which looked out to the street, was made of transparent glass, but even a child could just press a button to replace it for a wallscreen, or to switch on the holo images, or to put out the lights. John, however, was falling asleep and did not feel like fiddling around. His mother was happy: "A nice home…and cheap, also." She would put John to bed and go to the party.

The streets were awash with holographic lights, flowers, stars. In the great Sigma hall, the ceiling was teeming with butterflies of every possible color. The women wore electronic gemstone flowers on their hair and arms. The flowers opened and closed in sync with their breathing, releasing a pleasant scent. Cute little robots buzzed about. President Sam Nottobe was beaming. Yes, the Panslavian president would arrive soon; no, he had not received any official notification; Omar Miaulis did indeed have a lot of work to do, he kept repeating to the journalists without ever losing his nerve. Some reporters kept saying this was the Government's and Sigma's silver wedding.

Out in the country, some former Byorn citizens were setting up tents. Only a few people had left for Mars, and there weren't enough houses for everybody.

The new dome cast a faint pearl-like glow in the middle of the night as New Byorn's first party took place.

▲

At work, Anaiz was on edge. Thinking of Weber spying on her and Gorka's attacks sent her head spinning. An hour passed before she gave in to turning on the enquiry terminal, her hands shaking. Wait! It didn't respond. Had they cut her power? Maybe Weber had reported her? Luckily, with her hand on the keyboard, Anaiz realized she was being silly — she had typed the title "Coastal contamination" before hitting the **Link/Break** button. *I'm such a terrible investigator. And maybe absent-minded, too. What if I'm wrong?* It didn't matter. Thinking she had to break the cycle, she linked the terminal and paid attention to the words as she typed them. Then, she carefully read down to the last section title:

```
          COASTAL CONTAMINATION ■
                   INDEX
    1.   LIST AND HISTORY OF CONTAMINATED TOWNS
    2.   MAPS AND STATISTICS
    3.   CAUSES
    4.   EFFECTS
    5.   MEANS OF CONTAMINATION
              5.1 AIR
              5.2 LAND
              5.3 WATER
    6.   THE USE OF WALLS TO COUNTERACT COASTAL CONTAMINATION
    7.   MATERIALS THAT COUNTERACT COASTAL CONTAMINATION
             (SELECT SECTION AND PRESS SEND) ■
```

Anaiz already knew about sections 1 and 2. She had no need for 3, 4, or 5. She requested section 6. There she accessed documents she had already seen long ago, related to V-schools and colleges. Anaiz requested technical details by hitting "guide," and the screen brought up the old documents' titles. She kept pressing **Continue** for a while. Soon she realized that, even as she used a fast-reading method, the screen took longer and longer to fill. There was no doubt: neither hyperglass nor the dome were mentioned anywhere.

FOR A NEW QUERY PLEASE RETURN TO INDEX

The words remained flashing in the bottom line of the message.

▲

There was a gap in the data. Anaiz snapped back to attention as she noticed she had been staring blankly at those words. Her fingers quickly hit the **Index** button: she was certain that the dome did not appear mentioned anywhere in the index. Not to mention hyperglass. In which section could the purposes of hyperglass be found, then? The Sigma engineers had to put their documents somewhere in the database!

No dome in the "Coastal contamination" section, that was for sure.

And in the "Dome" section, no hyperglass to be found. Hyperglass might have a separate index for itself. So it must be more important for the New Byorn mission than she thought.

▲

Sam Nottobe, president of the United States of the World, was daydreaming in front of the map of Earth. The map showed the consequences of World War Three: countries colored in blue, purple, black, yellow, red, and white. The old Soviet Union, Central and Eastern Europe, that is, Panslavia, were purple. Indonesia was black. India, blue. Yellow marked Africa (except for Maghreb), Madagascar, Japan, and China, which controlled them all. The two Americas and Western Europe were a red hue. President Nottobe smiled bitterly. United states, they may be. But that "of the World" was nothing but an old dream. No one had tried to steal the title from them, though.

The president's eyes rested on the white countries: Iran, the Arab Countries, the Middle East, and Spain had become the "White Eagle" nations. Iran, thanks to its abundance in minerals, was becoming increasingly imperialistic. Its economy, too. These days you could find goods "made in Iran" anywhere. Iranian planes had been seen treading Indian airspace five or six times now, but whenever a Panslavian plane did the same, China and Iran called their ambassadors back to national soil. The White Eagle was gladly turning into a cuckoo. Nottobe switched off the illuminated map. A blue wall took its place. The president turned on the microphone on his desk.

"Official message. Official message. Send to wallscreens. The USW government repeats its refusal to accept any more Iranians in Perpignan's vicinity. Those who are found will be captured and declared 'persona non grata.' Over." Hopefully the threats would whet Iran's appetite for war.

A ping. A robotic voice came out of the desk. "Official report. Official report. The Indian government has fallen under pressure of Iranian forces. Panslavia has sent an ultimatum to Iran. Official report. Should it be broadcast by holovision, Mr. President?" Nottobe's expression darkened. As he spoke a few words on autopilot, he pressed the **Space** bar three times: the news was sent to the holovision. "Already? Too soon."

He had no time to waste. He typed in a number. Another office appeared. Behind the desk a big, bald man: Natanael Opusday, "Mr. Sigma." Nottobe was anxious, but this man seemed the picture of calm, as if the latest events meant nothing to him.

"Good afternoon, Opusday. It's time we initiate plan 3."

The bald man did not ask any questions.

"Excellent, Mr. Nottobe."

"And, about what you said yesterday—"

"It still stands. You can be sure we have no doubts."

"See you soon, then."

As Opusday's face faded out, Nottobe noticed a red light blinking on his table: the "holo-red" that was a direct link between the presidential offices in Moscow and New York. He waited a little before brushing the holo-red button with a clammy hand. A 20th-century library appeared. Omar Miaulis, the Panslavian president, was a book enthusiast and never used terminals except for work. Nottobe watched Miaulis's pitch black, smiling eyes in his Cherkess face. Same as always. It was impossible to tell what he was feeling.

"Sooner than expected, eh, pal?" Miaulis said.

"It's your decision. At your word."

"The Iranians have 'knocked down' two Panslavian planes. Or, better said…" Miaulis's hands caressed a yatagan. *That's not an office, it's a museum,* Nottobe thought. *It'll be hard for him to leave it behind.* "…two or indeed *three* planes. And a bunch of soldiers have walked out of that third plane."

They're not micromissiles, they're men! And men can be talked to.

"Infantry," Miaulis continued. "Just like in the old days. And, officially, they're now 'sightseeing' in the country."

"What can we do if they happen to get into a bit of a quarrel with some local thieves? It's their problem…"

Miaulis put his yatagan and his smile abruptly away.

"Also, Sam, we'd like to know the limits of your support."

"You got it started quite early. But now that you have, we need to get on with plan 3."

Miaulis's shoulders lowered a little. He had missed part of what Nottobe had just said.

"Er, I'll see you tomorrow, then. Goodbye."

In Teheran, the president of Iran was also looking at the map of Earth. Reza Ayatollah's soldiers were fighting in India, but the new Indian government had called on the UN for the Blue Robots to throw the fighters out of the country. The Ayatollah had been shocked by that decision, convinced that all Indians were too busy drowning in fear. Reza's fine, dark features seemed peaceful, but anger grew inside him the more he thought about the fact that he hadn't taken India — the gate to Indonesia — early enough. Now it was all in the hands of the UN.

THE TRUTH

A LOUD SIGNAL rang as Anaiz hastily walked into the building. What now? Ah, yes, she was still holding her electronic card. She threw it into the pigeonhole's mobile basket. *I should call Weber. If not, he'll think I have run away and will be spying on me again*, she thought, running into the elevator so fast that she almost hit her head on the back wall. "I need time to search," she said to herself.

She videophoned Weber from her office. *I'll ask him what he wants, if there's any work for me.* The videophone didn't display the engineer's handsome face. He had activated the answering machine. "Mr. Weber has been summoned to an urgent meeting. He will be away all morning. You have 3 minutes to leave a message. I repeat. Mr. Weber has been summoned to an urgent meeting…" Since she had to leave a message, she said she had next weekend free. *I sound so silly*, she thought, *but Jep thinks I'm madly in love with him, so he'll believe my being all lovey-dovey.*

So this meant there was no Weber to watch what she was up to. And she didn't have much work to turn in. She was already sitting in front of the terminal. First she turned on the typer; she'd need to make a list to remember the documents she was going to request from the computer. She'd type into the printer. Yes. No! She must leave no trace. She'd just write it down and be ready to take everything with her.

What titles had she requested already? "Coastal contamination." Useless. "Dome." Also useless. The "Coastal contamination" section didn't mention any domes or hyperglass. No hyperglass either in the "Dome" section. She quickly hit the **Remove** button on the typer. The screen went blank. Perfect: no trace.

Anaiz wrote a line at the beginning of her work document, so if anybody came in they would believe her busy at work. She had to request the hyperglass section. She'd need to dial on the S0 computer. There was actually a section on hyperglass—there *had* to be, she'd worked on the damn thing! Anaiz requested it and the section appeared on her screen.

```
        ▲
┌─────────────────────────────┐
│         HYPERGLASS          │
│     ------------------      │
│          INDEX ■            │
│   1.  Components            │
│   2.  Properties           │
│   3.  Uses                 │
│       3.1 Dome             │
│       3.2 Others           │
│       3.3 Technical details│
└─────────────────────────────┘
```

She was startled by the sound of footsteps in the corridor. She sat up, looking at the door. Her hand was right next to the **Link/Break** button, ready to delete everything. No, the footsteps were fading. Anaiz requested title number 1. A sentence in red appeared, blinking, on the screen:

PROVIDE YOUR CODE ■

Anaiz typed 00.202730.15.1524. The screen lit up yellow. The S0 database quickly showed her the document. It was interesting to see the parts she hadn't done. But even those didn't teach her anything new. Then she requested section 3.3. Again the red band of text:

PROVIDE YOUR CODE ■

Once again, Anaiz sent her personal number to S0. A different sentence appeared.

YOUR REQUEST WAS INCORRECT, REPEAT REQUEST ■

RETURN TO INDEX FOR INFORMATION ON OTHER SECTIONS

The young archigrapher pressed **Correct** and asked again.

YOUR REQUEST WAS INCORRECT, REPEAT REQUEST ■

Anaiz deleted everything and asked again for the Hyperglass section. *Let's see. I've pressed **Send**, haven't I? Yep. My code.* She went through the numbers in her code again. *Then **Send** and title 3.3. **Send** again. The screen is yellow, so I have called S0, and I'm definitely linked to it.*

A red line was unfolding on the screen.

YOUR REQUEST WAS INCORRECT, REPEAT REQUEST ■

A blue line of text was also coming in. So slow.

RETURN TO INDEX FOR INFORMATION ON OTHER SECTIONS

She tried to input the title first, then her code. She hit **Send**. Again that message.

▲

Anaiz tried to formulate her question in every possible order imaginable, using every key. It was hopeless. She was sure she had done everything right. The old S0 database just wouldn't give her the data. She had never heard of a database refusing to answer. Two things could be happening: either there was something wrong with S0 or else there wasn't. But when a computer didn't bring anything up, it used to be considered a false response, and it seldom happened. Normally, if an internal circuit burned out, a small light appeared on screen until S0 brought the system back up. But she had never seen this happen.

If S0 was in order, it was denying her that document. She asked again. Since when was it using that error sentence? she wondered as she input her code. Could the answer be a secret, barred to her? She was fuming. *After all the hard work I've done for them, they treat me like I'm some kind of thief. Is it because I'm Bask? But that's why they chose me in the first place! If I were the president.... Yeah, if I—* Her thoughts halted. She unlinked the terminal, her heart racing. She suddenly noticed the deafening silence around her. And the fearful silence inside her. She sat like this for a long time, white as a sheet, her face buried in her hands. Her thoughts were awakening, swirling, breaking in waves until they drove her crazy, jumping faster than the answers in a computer, blinking in and out like silicon fleas: the president, the peace talks, the president apparently coming to New Byorn, the president in New Byorn already, Sigma, hyperglass, Weber's pleasing body, "Talking shop on a weekend? Let's go dance!", the overlook...Hyperglass, secrets, the locals thrown out, Gorka's attacks, Baldi! The New Byorn shelter, New Byorn for Sigma members.... The Panslavian president just arrived in New Byorn, Weber disconnecting the terminal— because he knew something.

At last, Anaiz stood up, very slowly. Her body felt as if it belonged to an old woman, heavy and hard. She felt aged.

She understood the truth.

THE VIRTUAL CONFERENCE

Like every other villa in New Byorn, Sam Nottobe's had a conservatory or sun room. To be precise, it was an electronic forest that cast both light and heat. The forest was not in plain sight; rather, the rays of light came "naturally" out of the ceiling and corners. The small room was located in the middle of the house. A small paradise glowing in bluish warmth, or completely dark, where music may or may not play—everybody could choose their own atmosphere. That afternoon, the light in that conservatory was blue. Inside it, two famous men, completely naked, lying on viscose beds, stared at a wall. Nottobe's stomach rose and fell in synch with the relaxation program, but Miaulis wouldn't calm down. At last, they heard the loud "click" they had been waiting for. The room switched off, and the 3D images of three men appeared in its place: Nala Gandhi, the Indian president, Reza Ayatollah, and the Indonesian leader. Then the rest of faces showed up one by one. The remote peace talks had begun.

India spoke first. Nala Gandhi had black wavy hair, large, deep black eyes, and the smooth, hard expression of a Shiva sculpted in stone. He spoke with a gentle voice.

"Despite India's neutrality, two foreign countries are escalating their dispute *manu militari* in our territory. We request before all attendees of this congress that they remove their forces and issue an official apology." As he spoke, he remembered a quote from Bhagavad Gita. No warrior wanted a young fighter against a blind king.

"Sorry!" Miaulis shouted back to Gandhi. "Let's apologize to our fellow country here, neutral India. We should be throwing some light on a different debate, anyway. If all Indians, just like every other nation's population, have the right to elect their government, we'd like to understand the current situation." Miaulis relaxed his tone. "The Indian government has been replaced by a new one. And in the meantime two Panslavian aircrafts have been taken down. By whom? India? No, India recognizes and approves our presence. We have recorded the last message sent from one of the planes. There is no doubt—the Iranians destroyed them! In Indian air space! Two men survived the accident, and one was taken prisoner by Iranian *foot soldiers*. In India! Where's Indian neutrality in this? Where is Iran, which we have graciously accepted on European soil, in Spain, within our borders? Will Iran now say that it's all been some thrill-seeking soldiers' stupidity? I sure hope so."

Nala Gandhi stood up slowly.

"If these two countries refuse to stop waging war on our soil, India will declare their attitude hostile and will ask the UN for help in order to find the path to peace." As he pronounced the word *peace*, he gave them a gentle smile. What had to be said was now said.

Reza's image was moving constantly, so much so that it was difficult to catch his face. He was sitting in a red armchair by his marble swimming pool, in khaki military shorts, legs dipped in the water. The armchair kept moving here and there. His words, on the other hand, he delivered loud and clear:

"So now we have to pay off someone else's debt. Mr. Nala Gandhi believes that we have trodden on neutral Indian territory. And Mr. Miaulis would like to make it seem like we are the big bad wolf. I also shall make a few comments. First of all: that poor little Panslavian plane flying through India and whose crew we captured was, as it seems, a *military* aircraft. If anybody would like to know where India's neutrality lies, you might want to ask Panslavia. Second of all: they haven't said a word about the Panslavian 'tourists' peeking on our uranium mines. And yet, what about the Iranian tourists that have been kicked out of Perpignan by Mr. Nottobe?"

Five minutes later, the virtual conference showed no signs of progress. The Chinese, Indonesian, and USW presidents carried on separately. Miaulis took a couple of pills and went for a break in one of the rooms in the villa. After, all image and sound was automatically switched off for the following hour, so that each president could gather their citizens' opinions via computer. At least, officially. Each of them had to retire to a secret place, from which they would remotely cast their vote. No world leader knew the location of the others. The machines used to hold remote conferences were small and light, easy to carry anywhere. But each president had the right to either be by themselves or with another leader. That had been Nottobe's and Miaulis's choice. Not a single human hand took part in the voting system's technical arrangement. Everything was done by software. In that respect, therefore, no one could spy on anyone else's vote.

▲

The voting took place automatically, an hour later, with the video off.

Lao Hito, the Chinese president, thinking that he would gladly "Chinafy" India, took a false book from a cabinet in his office. He then pressed a button in the book: **I**. He had cast his vote. The leader of Indonesia voted from an elegant wooden palace. Wishing for the big bad wolves to go ahead and eat each other, he pressed **I**. Nottobe walked to the small pool by the conservatory. He sank his hand into the water and pressed a button on the pool wall before returning to the sun room, where he said to Miaulis, who was waiting for him, "È finita la commedia." He had pressed number **I**. Miaulis sighed. Squatting in a Kali temple, Nala Gandhi saw the result of the UN's decision. In front of him, above the screen, the black depiction of Kali, teeth sharp, surrounded by skulls. *Click*. A blinking red star appeared on the screen, the signal preceding an official announcement. Then the words started appearing, one by one. White words on red bands extended line by line. The red star kept blinking.

> OFFICIAL ANNOUNCEMENT. OFFICIAL ANNOUNCEMENT.
>
> THE UN HAS REJECTED INDIA'S CALL
>
> THE UN REMOTE CONFERENCE HAS UNANIMOUSLY CONDEMNED INDIA
>
> FOR A NATION MORE CONCERNED WITH ITS OWN PEACE THAN WITH
>
> GLOBAL CONFLICTS DENOTES A SELFISH AND RACIST INCLINATION

Nala thought of the Mahabharata. "A blind king—and now us, his children, must pierce our own eyes." He cried for a long time, staring at the image of Kali. He didn't care; he was alone. Afterwards, he did a little yoga before making for the keyboard to spread the news.

From New Byorn, Miaulis blocked UN negotiations.

Nottobe declared that the USW would enter the war by Panslavia's side.

The theatrics were over.

▲

Gorka's front door made of wood and hinges was ajar. A recognizable racket of voices came from inside. Anaiz knew it well: a local meeting. Everybody was arguing. She didn't find Baldi in the house. Anaiz hesitated for a moment. Where to start? She had begun to understand that she had only done the easiest part. Her "escape" from the office had actually been as momentous as a walk in the park. Nobody had paid any attention to her. Not in the corridors, even less at the ovamobile station. *Well, I don't have "I know the truth" written across my face anyway and Sigma members don't have time now to worry about a simple archigrapher. That could well be more proof that I have discovered the truth. When they need me, they'll realize I'm gone. And maybe they'll leave me alone.*

The ovamobile had taken her to the town square. She had made straight for Baldi's house. Nobody was in. She had been too afraid to go to her parents' home. *If they do look for me, they'll videophone there.* She had thought of finding Baldi. She knew the boy had been secretly in love with her for a long time.

Not finding Baldi anywhere, she had made the hardest decision: going to Gorka's house. When she got there, she was startled by a thin, black-haired woman who came out of the half-open door.

"Anaiz, how come you're here?"

Anaiz was unable to reply. She was sure Gorka had been giving her a terrible reputation.

"What's wrong, Anaiz?" the woman continued. "You're short of breath and half crying!"

"Please, Maialen," Anaiz said between ragged breaths. "No time…to waste. I want to see Gorka right now."

"He's quite angr—"

"I need to see him."

Maialen went back in, talking to herself, and quickly returned accompanied by Gorka. Anaiz noticed a few white hairs on his head. She also saw he was tired; he looked 50. His darkened face betrayed no emotion. His words, however, did:

"What's going on? But first of all, how did you know we were having a meeting?"

"That one's easy. I didn't know. I've come because I needed to see you."

Gorka smirked.

"Has Sigma sent you here to talk?"

"No. I quit my job forever this morning."

A silence. Anaiz noticed the fine lines on Gorka's forehead.

"After finding out what I know now," she continued, "I don't want to work with people like that."

"What did you find out?" asked Gorka.

"The reason why Sigma has thrown so many locals out of New Byorn."

"Everybody knows that! So that they could hand their homes to Sigmans!"

"There's something else, Gorka. Please, let's not waste time. I need to talk to everybody this instant."

Shock showed in Gorka's blue eyes for the first time. The man took Anaiz by the arm.

"But you're white as a sheet! What is it?"

"I need everybody to hear it."

"Come with me."

Everyone rolled their eyes as Anaiz came in. Gorka called for silence, before saying "Go ahead, Anaiz, talk to them."

"I have found out what the dome is actually for. Sigma hasn't told the full truth. I searched for the properties of hyperglass, and the computer refused to give me the details. I had to provide my code to see the document. Even then, I got no response."

"So you don't know a thing, then!"

Anaiz ignored Gorka's outburst. She continued, almost shouting now: "Yes, I do! I have guessed it thanks to what I already knew! Hyperglass isn't only useful against coastal contamination. It can stop radiation too! That's why Sigma has covered New Byorn with the dome. That's why they have installed so many new computers there. That's why the most famous experts of the USW and Panslavia have been invited to live there. In times of peace, the New York computers work fine for all of Europe. At war, though, the connections may be severed. That's why the computers had to be placed under the dome. That's why they've bought so much food they didn't need from the farmers: they had to stock up for later. That's why they gave locals false figures about coastal contamination, so that they would accept the dome to be installed on their lands—they didn't expect anyone to be looking for the numbers under a different index in a computer. I have been unknowingly feeding you these lies."

She heard a gasp of shock. That was when she noticed Baldi in the room.

"Listen, Anaiz...when did you realize there was low risk of contamination from the coast? Was it when you saw the actual figures?"

"No. I saw a friend behaving strangely, and that got me thinking."

"You mean Weber, don't you?"

Anaiz saw Baldi's sad smile and felt embarrassed. Gorka hit the table with his fist.

"What's this Weber nonsense?" Gorka looked at Baldi's expression and stopped. "Well. Come on, Baldi, enough with the chatter!"

"When I learned that the president would come to inaugurate the New Byorn dome, I was sure."

Anaiz's father spoke.

"Don't worry so much, dear. What you just told us is all just speculation!"

"Sorry, dad, but—"

Clicks and pings interrupted the argument. All the micro-radios in people's wrists had turned on automatically. The Aida trumpets rang loud, signaling that an official call was coming in. Everybody went silent, their hearts racing.

"Official announcement. Official announcement. The USW and Panslavian governments have declared war on Iran. Here follows a list of official messages—"

"You were right, Anaiz," Gorka acknowledged, and hushed the crowd.

"Next message: All Sigma members from Team A 1001 must return to New Byorn before noon. I repeat: All Sigma members from Team A 1001…"

Gorka stood up. He suddenly looked younger, lighter.

"Turn off the radios!" he called. "Off to Byorn, everybody! Anaiz and Baldi will videophone the mayors in the other towns. We need a group of people to bring as many ovamobiles as possible back here. Who will do it?"

"I will!"

"Us, too!"

"And then, we'll all go to Byorn! That shelter is ours, too. We will not be left out to die by radiation or hunger!"

▲

It was 11:30 when everybody began to evacuate their towns, most of them by ovamobile, some on foot. They grabbed any transport they found on the way. They also took every single laser saw they could find. They carried sticks in their hands. Some had sacks full of stones.

Anaiz carefully put a videophone on her arm. She stood up to open the window. The sound of turmoil outside seeped into the living room. As she pressed the **Window** button again, she heard a "Hello" behind her.

She saw Gorka standing at the door.

"No one has responded from New Byorn for quite a while," Anaiz said, half falling onto a chair. She expected a *You have no right to be tired*, or something like that, from him, but it never came. Gorka was on a break. His blue eyes looked at Anaiz but didn't see her. Still, he nodded when she told him that everybody had been informed. She thought of how handsome he had looked when he was giving instructions to people at the meeting. Now he looked again like he used to: his dark-skinned face, fine wrinkles drawn by life's fingers in the corners of his eyes and lips; his sad mouth: a wiry man, young still, standing straight despite the wounds life had dealt on him. When Anaiz said that telecommunications from Byorn had already been cut, hope seeped out of him, slowly, almost lovingly.

He looked at the woman. It was clear that she also had understood. As Anaiz's eyes rested on the man's hands, covered in copper hair, a pang of shame woke him. This woman could have easily been in the New Byorn shelter by now.

"Anaiz, I just wanted to say…Erm, you having been a Sigman and all—"

"Here we go again, Sigma this and Sigma that! What have I done to you?"

In spite of himself, Gorka gave her a timid smile.

"Anaiz, please, listen! The ovamobiles are Sigma property, aren't they? What are we going to do? They might actually know what we're up to right now."

Anaiz stood up, walking towards Gorka.

"We'd better go there, anyway. We should do something, anything. But don't mention Sigma to me ever again, Gorka. I will never forgive you if you do."

Gorka blushed, surrender on his face.

"Deal. You deserve peace." A shadow crossed his expression. "I'm sure there's a spot for you in Baldi's ovamobile."

"I'd rather go with you."

Gorka opened his mouth, closed it again, smiling weakly. Forgetting his pride, he embraced Anaiz in a sudden move.

"Anaiz, forgive—"

Anaiz's kiss kept him quiet long enough to make him lose the courage to say he was too old for her.

Then Anaiz, as abrupt as Gorka — perhaps fearing what he might say next — unlinked her arms from around him and walked out with a loud "Come on." Gorka followed her without a word. Anaiz's kiss had done him good.

▲

The silver-colored shells of the ovamobiles hovered over the old roads, the men and women inside them wearing menacing or fearful expressions, the children, amazement. The people walking at the edge of the road carried viscose bags on their backs, a sign that they had found the time to pack a few essential items. Weber looked for Anaiz's face among the crowd, unsuccessfully. He gave up — he had other things to do. As people came in, they approached in groups; nobody seemed to be losing their minds. Maybe because most of them had lived through World War Three.

Weber looked at the screen. The code K-10 was blinking on it. "So close already?" he exclaimed, remembering that he was standing in the main screen room of New Byorn. On the screen, the rural inhabitants of the Bask Country were getting closer all the time. Weber typed on the keyboard, requesting their speed: as the computer calculated that they would be in New Byorn before noon, a red signal turned on with a faint beep. Weber was growing increasingly nervous.

What? Them already? What am I supposed to do? I'm supposed to be opening doors now, too? Well, I can't leave them *outside....* The young engineer looked at the door. Three red lights had blinked on. It meant that three people were behind it. The camera outside the door turned on, and the small screen connected to it displayed a bald head shining under the lights. Weber also recognized a famous black moustache and a hawkish nose. He pressed a red button. The door, round, dark green, and with a 2 displayed above, opened with a light hiss. Misters Natanael Opusday, Omar Miaulis, and Sam Nottobe came out of it.

K-7: the screens showed an entire country organized in groups that were constantly getting closer, ready to break into New Byorn. "You can't record their voices?" Opusday asked.

"We can, sir. These images are being recorded by an invisible spy microsatellite. The sound can be turned on if you wish." Weber typed in a number.

"TO BYORN! TO BYORN! WE WANT TO LIVE!"

Miaulis bit his thumb. Opusday sat down and said, "Take the sound off. What's the point?" The numbers were back on the screens, declaring K-7. Those people were already just 7 km away from New Byorn. Opusday stood up again. "They want to come in just like that. Don't fret: they won't. I don't know how they found out, but even if somebody has given us away, you can be sure that it doesn't matter at all at this point. Mr. Nottobe?"

The screen marked K-5. Nottobe, with his back to the others, was hitting a different keyboard. On another screen, a map of New Byorn (now that the city had become a circle, it was easy to read) clearly showed that there was not a soul next to the dome wall.

"There's nobody," Nottobe said, smiling.

Opusday smiled back.

"Of course not, Mr. Nottobe, fear not! That's because we have taken all citizens to the old underground shelters. They'll know about the dome later on. In the meantime, they won't see what will happen outside."

"And what about the whistleblower? The country folk must have found out from someone! Whoever betrayed us must be outside, and we stopped external communications a while ago, except for the ones you're seeing, of course. We left inter-town communications on…Weber, wake up! You've got them at K-4 already."

"Look," Miaulis shouted, startling the other three men. "Look, Sam! On your small screen. There's people outside! Some haven't gone into the shelter."

Nottobe looked at the city map.

"What do you mean, Omar? Those stars, the green blinking ones? No, those are robots covering up the dome wall from the inside. Thanks to them, the New Byorners won't see outside."

"Well, fine. But wait! Look there. A red star is blinking."

The four men began to work on the computers. Opusday's fat fingers moved fast as flies hopping from button to button. He sent some robots in search for that unidentified person.

"K-3, Weber!"

"Calm down, Omar. Our Weber will take care of them."

The engineer looked up.

"With all due respect, Mr. President, I don't have the right to make such decisions. That pertains to you. This is the button you're supposed to press."

Nottobe stationed himself in front of the computer Weber pointed at, paying no attention the man's pale countenance.

"What about the person by the wall?"

"Never mind that; the robots will find them soon."

▲

Somebody was indeed by the dome wall, at a spot where one could still see through, far from all the robots. That person wasn't Iranian, nor a Sigman, nor a spy, nor a whistleblower. His name was Ganix, and he did not know what the dome was for. His eyes were glassy, due perhaps to shock or because he had been crying, his lips touching the hyperglass. He was a seven-year-old boy. He had run away when everybody was taken to the shelters. He just *wouldn't* go in there. He hadn't known what was going on, but he knew now that the farmers were angry, and he was there to see them — or better said, he just accidentally happened to be seeing them. In the shelter, his mother and aunts were videophoning, desperate to find the boy. But Ganix just kept staring at people's faces as if at something forbidden…

▲

"K-2, Mr. President. Your call!"

The president of the USW pushed a red circle.

Then the lost boy saw it all unfold from the other side of the hyperglass. He recognized his cousin, Libe, and shouted at her. It was hopeless. Suddenly everything changed: the people were being knocked down as they approached. Everybody on the front line was falling over as if they had hit something with their heads.

Then they stood up, and the men who tried to shoot lasers at the dome fell down again, their faces and bodies covered in blood. The boy couldn't hear any sound. Short of breath, he could only see mouths opening and closing. He couldn't find Libe any more. Somebody was yelling into a megaphone. People were trying to flee in any way they could, leaving the injured—were they injured, or…? Ganix didn't want to know—on the ground. The boy would have plenty to wonder about for many years. That day, his childhood had left him forever.

In the main screen room, Weber turned off the terminals. A brief silence fell among the four men.

"They're gone. The force field has done a beautiful job pushing them away," Nottobe commented.

A robot found the boy crying by the wall and easily carried him to the shelter infirmary.

"The dome and the force field have proven their worth," Opusday said.

▲

In India, neither side made any progress using old-fashioned weaponry. So they moved on to micromissiles and small nuclear bombs. First, Panslavia bombarded Palestine. In Jerusalem, no stone was left on top of another. In the afternoon of that same day, Iran sent micromissiles to Retrograd, the Lithuanian capital. The surrounding peatlands were saturated with radiation.

A flower of fire. The sculptures of Bahabalipuram, the elegant Taj Mahal, Angkor Thom—they were now nothing but memories. Shiva swallowed India whole and ripped Parvati's tender breast to shreds.

A mushroom cloud of smoke. Never again would Rio have a carnival. In Isfahan, as the roses of radio bloomed, all women wore death on their faces. No more blue Masurian lakes.

All Sigmans were in New Byorn, where the government had also gathered many industrialists and experts.

In the Americas and most of Europe, it was the apocalypse. All intercontinental radio broadcasts were shut down. Many were left homeless, and hopeless. South America was on fire. New York city's antipollution wall was destroyed.

New Byorn remained whole under the hyperglass, shiny as a pearl.

Choppy Water

To all Katryls

THE MORNING KATRYL fled from Holylight to Shuripi, the spaceport lake sparkled and splashed under the blue sun. The boy, eyes sun-blue, shiny with fever in darkened sockets, stood on the conveyor bridge transporting him, looking at the city's blue houses carved into azurite slopes. The penetrating smell of the waterways, like salt linden blossom, rose to his nostrils. Katryl had now left behind the roboguards that walked noiselessly around the spaceport quay dressed in those strange red suits, the thin crack in their foreheads that was an electronic third eye clicking open and closing again.

If they had a picture of me, they would have caught me a long time ago. They've looked up the number I've got on my neck and... not a word. Maybe it's because I stepped off a private hovercraft.

Suddenly, Katryl's hurting body felt dizzy. No, not dizzy. It was planet Turion's warm earth under his feet, shaking.

"A 2 on the Richter scale, I'd say; the first today," the old man beside him said in Neobask. "If we Shuripians had as much money as we have little earthquakes.... Oh, well. Every place has its own kind of trouble."

Katryl, surprised to be spoken to, acted as if he had not heard the man, but stole a glance at him to make sure he was just a chatty fellow. *No. There's no vertical line on his forehead. He can't be robopol. That slow pace is just him being old. I mustn't get paranoid. Here, too, on the equator, in Neobaskia, I will be living among my compatriots. Even if it's been eight centuries since the people from planets Basik and Kobol landed on Turion and, dividing the equatorial region — Neobaskia, our country — into two, took one half each.*

The truth was that the spaceport was full of foreigners, and nobody was paying attention to him. Everyone moved about in silence with microaurals in their ears, listening to cassettes while driving or working, which made Katryl, who was empty-eared, easy to identify by the friend awaiting him.

Meanwhile, in a quiet Holylight office, a file card appeared on the terminal screen:

■   NAME: Jonle Ondor

Blood type: A RH-

Height: 1.80 m

Hair: Black

Eyes: Sun blue

Unusual marks: 0

Born in Holylight 10/12/3505. 23 yo

Family: Father interned 3 years in Medipolitical Center n° 44, no cure, deceased 03/08/3520

Brother dead by gunshot in the action against the Aire missile factory

Notes: Interned 9 days in 3528 in Medipolitical Center n° 41 ■

Charged: No

MARKED: Yes, hallucinol

Neobask speaker: Yes

Potentially dangerous: Yes   ■

In Shuripi, at the lake quay, a short, dark-skinned boy of about twenty years ran to Katryl and quietly put his hand on his shoulder. Katryl offered him a soft, timid smile.

"I'm Azir." He pointed at a blue hillside, covered in carven windows and doors. "That's where you'll live. Over the Iber waterway. Let's go to the boat."

A piercing pain twisted Katryl's face as he dropped into the vessel with a splash.

"Katryl, did they use radio?"

"Yes."

"The house is up there—yeah, I know. You'll have a hard time going up. A friend has given us a microsyringe in secret. I'll take care of you."

Katryl nodded. Neither of them mentioned again what Katryl had endured. The rocking of the hyperlatex boat, which led them out of the lake and into the waterways, the smell of lodum, the choppy water, the people's voices, everything made Katryl giddy and dozy, waking a desire in him to dive into the city that offered him shelter as if into a small, warm sea.

◆

By the time Katryl found a job, he had already explored Shuripi to its very last corner. It was his hiding place, and it gladly offered him its waterways, wavy as strands of hair adorned with vessels; the blue houses of its caves, bluer than the sun, carved full of round windows and doors; and that heady aroma of salt linden blossoms. That night, like every night, the city of Shuripi rocked Katryl with its splashing water—even though that sound, like a dog's wobbly trot, frightened him at first—inside the warm, dark dwelling over the Iber waterway in which he lived with five other young men.

And, just like every morning, Shuripi woke him early with the sounds of the market and those on their way there. The sighing of the boat reactors, the shouting and singing of the people, his friend Azir's murmuring: everything reached his ears in a confusing mix.

Splish! Splash!

"To the right! How's your little daughter?" Splotch! "She's been crying all night, it's the teeth, you know..." "Go back to the quay and..." "Dum-durum..." Plop! "Watch out for the Crab!"

"This damn city!" Katryl rubbed his eyes, revealing a green square in his armpit: the cybernetic mark that officially distinguished intergalactic fugitives.

Outside, the market's clamor persisted.

"Hey, you! Bring the anchor over, the magnetic plate's here! Hey, Luxi! Long time…!"

Splosh! Brooooom!

"Look where you're going, you oaf! That's a pretty mark you've made on the flank! Left my boat trembling." "This one, this one!" "Nice and easy, Bipil. Pass me the rod, won't ya?"

◆

Cling, cling. Click-clickatick-click.

"Oy! Another one of those blasted earthquakes! Could be a 4!"

"Oh, I don't know, Azir…I'd say it was a 10, at the very least."

"Katryl, how about you stop mocking me and search instead? Where did my shaving razor go?"

"Azir, don't you understand that, shaved or not, you're still ugly as sin? Here it is, man."

The sweet chime of the calcite bell silenced them. Someone had knocked with the chiseled seahorse on the door. As Lor slowly walked to the door, Katryl crossed the room to push open the circular window, ready to jump. His fear was unfounded: the visitor was their neighbor, "Telepath" Mik—a Neobaskian and an ally.

"Katryl, I hear you're looking for a part-time job. Would you like to work at my tavern?"

"I'd be glad to. If I'm to get on an aircraft to Delta, I have to put the money together."

Azir was restless.

"It's your best choice. You already know what happened to Arl and Kep, right?"

Katryl did know, all too well: that fragrant ambush that was Shuripi, the winding alleys between the waterways that could be hideouts or mortal traps, the ancient walls covered in crystallized drops of salty lodum. Yes, he did know the street where the Basik robopol spies had killed young Arl with microneedles, because every time he walked past that place he saw Arl's name written in black hydroglyphs, forever glazed over the warm earth with lava spray. He also knew the blackened glaze crab of Oberon quay, where they had blown up his friend Kep's boat. Those wonderful hydroglyphs…. The only written words on planet Turion, since Kobol and Basik wrote nothing but numbers and crosses. Hydroglyphs — impossible to scratch away. Katryl said, "If the Basik robopol have followed me, too, all the way here…. It's horrible, dying and having to leave your mark! I'd better fly to Delta as soon as I can."

In a quiet Holylight office, the telesecretary pressed a blue button to mark Jonle Ondor's file with a red star, signaling that Katryl had quietly stolen away from the city and from Basik.

◆

The day he noticed the bald man, Katryl was on the Great Waterway's garden-bridge. He saw him, dressed in a white sweater-tunic, through the wrinkled blades of esparto grass, and it seemed to him that the man was stealthily following him. Katryl suddenly turned right, toward the quay, but the man kept close, silently, following him. Katryl walked into a lychee wine shop. After a while, he stepped out and saw the man had disappeared…. No: there he was, by a small boat, crouched over, as if waiting for somebody. Katryl hardly felt the soft tremor of an earthquake — 2 on the scale, at most. The bald man seemed to almost trip and finally fell over the dock. Katryl ran until he came to the house next door to his, strode up the stairs and realized it was the wrong building. Too late to go back now. On the fourth floor, Katryl recognized a friend's front door and lightly knocked on it with the calcite sea-horse in its center.

"Hi, Katryl! What's up?"

"Let me in! And you haven't seen me, got it?"

"This way."

Shuripi's fourth floors had "rooftops" — or, better said, balconies — sculpted into the azurite. Katryl stepped through the window and jumped from one rooftop to the next, the way all Shuripi's children did since they were very small, until he reached his bedroom's round window. There, he scratched the wood with his finger until Azir opened it.

"Did they find you, or something?"

Both men looked down: on the quay, a bald man was noiselessly walking away. On his forehead, a thin line: the robopol's "third eye," the opening that could be both a photographic device and a weapon.

"Katryl, this morning a robopol killed Raf in front of his house.... You've got to move out!"

"Don't worry. I lost him. I have to go back to the tavern. But look, if he catches me, I'll defend myself. They want us to feel afraid so that we'll put up with anything, so that we leave Neobaskia and they can waste the energy of our volcanoes on their micromissiles. They want our land. Koboldians want to build a giant micromissile plant on it; Basikans want to squander our volcanic energy on micromissile factories. But enough talking. I'll see you later!"

When he walked into the street, Katryl tasted the wind's warm body, an invisible body smelling of salt linden blossom, in his nose and mouth— The essence of Shuripi.

◆

The night Katryl's identity was discovered, the warm rain's dainty feet tapping on the ground amplified the splashing of Shuripi's waterways. Katryl was at Jos's, among friends. He was mimicking (or, rather, mocking) the nervous head shakes and convoluted expressions of the Basikan president.

"Understand. Yes—that's what those reactionary, loudmouth Neobaskians should do. They must understand that what we offer is what's best for them. That is, instead of wasting their time speaking in words, they should leave that to our politicians and learn to send messages with our 200-Sound System, work listening to Basikan cassettes, forsake their language, and seek work outside Neobaskia. We will bring them hot water when we build our plant." Katryl shook his head. "Yes, I know that even lacking power plants, Neobaskians can sell Iodum from their water to the Turionites as a painkiller and antibiotic, but the blockade is inevitable. Even if the drugs from other planets are more expensive, we can't break the deals made with them. It's the market!" The locals' laughter engulfed Katryl's voice. He shook his head like a white bear and continued. "The heart. Yes—Neobaskia could become the heart of this planet. How can we refuse the help that Koboldians are offering from the other side of the line of volcanic waste? They want to build a micromissile plant on their side of Neobaskia. They're doing their best to achieve it: they place factories outside Neobaskian territory, generating unemployment inside. And all this, for what?" Katryl's voice was trembling. "For a nice old intergalactic war to reach Neobaskia, that is, our very own planet Turion! We will finally gain the right to eliminate them. For that's my…pardon me, the ambition of Turion's dominant countries. According to intergalactic law, we can't kick Neobaskians out or set up more military structures in the area, as long as the Neobaskian population remains over five million. We abide by the law. It's not our fault if an illegal missile factory is built and our government finds out too late. They are to blame, those faint-hearted Neobaskians and those psychopaths who divert volcanic lava every night from their lava rivers into the factories! It is they who operate outside the law! That's why we send the ones we catch to the medipolitical centers, where, thanks to a process of reeducation, Neobaskians may leave their nonsense behind and become quiet, good-mannered Basikans…or, at least, quit doing any more harm…"

Katryl, bright-eyed, drunk on his own speech, had been moving backward, toward the door, until he hit someone with his shoulder. The warm, rainy air entering from the open door wet his cheek. In the waterway, raindrops slowly drifted away.

"Sorry—"

On the doorstep stood a woman that Katryl had noticed before around the tavern. She was tan and big, with an athletic body, and was wearing coveralls made of shiny green netting. Her black eyes were brimming with tears of laughter. It looked like she was leaving…. Why? Katryl peered shyly at her tan forehead, afraid to find a vertical line, but the skin was extremely smooth. She was a real woman, not a robotic photographer, he was sure of it now. Feeling Katryl's stare and guessing his suspicions, the woman reddened in annoyance, sat on the chair beside her, and openly glared at the boy's arm, looking for the mark of galactic fugitives. It was useless: she did not find that square green tattoo; Katryl refused to acknowledge he had it. They exchanged looks. Katryl held up the hair from his forehead to show her his seahorse, the traditional mark of Neobaskian men, and she choked, embarrassed.

Poor guy, she thought. He's an escapee, and here I am, scowling at him.

Telepath Mik, the tavern owner, whose gift had helped him read the hesitation/longing in Katryl's mind and the embarrassment/compassion in the girl's, approached them from behind, gathering their thoughts. In the young Holylighter's mind, this happened: a private smile, two human silhouettes face to face, hands wide open — a sign that the young woman could do him no harm. Then Mik said, "Hi, Zerune!" and went back to his table.

She understood she was supposed to say something then. The two of them began talking at the same time:

"You made me laugh." / "Can't you stay a little longer?"

Katryl's irritation melted instantly. The luminous smile that his friends knew so well was back.

"Yeah."

Zerune surrendered under that sweet smile. Katryl accepted a glass of lychee wine from one of his friends, who were buzzing after his speech. Suddenly, a slight earthquake made Zerune's and Katryl's glasses slide down the table. As Katryl tried to catch them, his hands touched Zerune's. Three on the Richter scale.

The very moment Katryl told Zerune his name, circuit no 321 in Holylight connected to robopol agent no 430:

◆

321	430
Ondor Jonle	Goes by Katryl
1.80 m	1.80 m
Black hair	Black hair
Sun-blue eyes	Sun-blue eyes
Born in Holyight 10/12/3050	About 22 yo
Fugitive	Recently arrived
Potentially dangerous	No official address
Hallucinol damage ■	■

The photo from Holylight (Katryl, bearded) responded down the circuit to the portrait in Shuripi (Katryl, beardless) until, on the screen, blinked the phrase:

KATRYL = JONLE ONDOR

◆

Katryl woke at dawn in Zerune's bed, in the old Shuribe neighborhood, which gave the city its name. Under the green sky dozed the charming chimneys of ancient times, the helmspeople's old living quarters. Zerune had recently rented a small living space in one of those natural towers on the sea's edge so she could meet Katryl unmolested. From the open round window drifted the sweet sigh of the tepid waves and, every now and then, a sound that could be the choppy waters of a distant waterway.

Katryl, eyes closed, covered in sweat, was whimpering and trying to set himself free from the arms that pinned him down, mumbling "Pat, Pat, they're choking me" repeatedly. Finally, he heard the woman's voice tenderly speaking to him.

"Katryl, my love. Wake up! It's me, Zerune." Katryl did not recognize the name, but calmed down as he felt a warm body against his naked skin.

"Where's Pat?"

"Pat? Who's that, Katryl?"

Vertigo. Katryl was falling into the depths of the abyss. No — it was no abyss. *This is a nightmare; I've got to open my eyes, but I can't. I'm choking, somebody's choking me, I don't—*

He struggled to open his eyes, shivering in the warm equatorial night. Someone — who? — covered him up to the chin with a sheet.

His blue eyes vaguely made out a restless face. "Zerune?"

"Oh, Katryl! You finally recognized me. How are you feeling, my love?"

"B-bad…. Cold…"

Zerune noticed Katryl's sweaty forehead and went to fetch some honey. On her way to the kitchen, she opened the valve that carried the heat from the volcanoes and placed a mug of shoat milk on the heater.

"Zerune, where are you?"

Katryl was as pale as a corpse.

"Seems like you need to raise your blood sugar. You scared me. You were having a terrible dream…"

Katryl's hand caught Zerune's wrist.

"I was. They injected me with that damned hallucinol…. Ah, I'm going mad. Don't call anyone."

Zerune took a full spoon to his lips.

"Here, have some seaweed honey. Open your mouth." Katryl swallowed with difficulty. Stroking his forehead, Zerune said: "You have to eat. I'm going to the kitchen. Rest!"

Katryl waited for her in complete silence. When she returned, Zerune tried to help him sit up, holding him by the arms, but he bent down whining and dropped into her lap, holding his hands to his lower belly.

"Oh…long time ago…Zerune, the limun sulfate, quick…"

Zerune loaded the painkiller into the electronic pistol. Katryl unintentionally shrank back when he saw the pistol, with its microsyringe's tiny needles, approaching his abdomen.

"Don't worry. The nightmares have gotten your muscles all stiff. What did they use on you?"

"Radio impellers. They used scanners to check how deep they could go."

"Ready?"

"Yeah. Don't worry, I won't move."

Fifteen minutes later, Katryl was feeling better. He was gobbling down a bunch of fishtree leaves and hungrily washing them down with a mug of shoat milk. Yawning, he rested the back of his head on Zerune's arm.

"Sleepy?"

"I'm still afraid of sleeping, because of the hallucinol."

"That hallucinol…what is it?"

"The Kobol robopol, when they can't manage to subdue the Neobaskians they capture, inject them with hallucinol to scare the others. The substance comes from planet Earth, apparently. They used it for cleaning, as a powder. Some kids accidentally ate it, and the doctors discovered that, to someone with low blood sugar, especially if they haven't eaten anything for a while, hallucinol can become an onirotrope — it provokes bad dreams."

"Yeah. It gives you nightmares…. Maybe they plant false memories in your head with hypnosis and 'reset' you, like they did to Jos and Barbi. You mentioned a Pat…"

"Could be."

Zerune understood that she should not ask about Pat.

Katryl, who had never been a moaner, tried to comfort Zerune.

"The pain's gone. Thank you so much. Don't be sad. If I pay more attention and eat whenever I need to, I won't get any more episodes like this one. I hadn't had nightmares in a long time. It's my fault."

"Don't say that."

"It really is, though. I got here late last night, I'd been running around all day and didn't find the time to even eat a sandwich."

"Why didn't you ask me to make you something to eat?"

"It was late, I wasn't hungry. I just wanted you. It had been weeks since we'd last seen each other and…" said Katryl, giving Zerune a blue sideways glance. "Zerune, I wanted to talk to you.

I'm not going to Delta. I'd rather live here, in Shuripi." His eyes shut. "Kiss…"

Katryl collapsed into sleep, his face covered by Zerune's tender kisses and warm droplets of rain.

In Shuripi's Great Waterway, a bald man dressed in a white sweater-tunic was aimlessly, stealthily pacing about. On his forehead was that vertical crevice that was constantly opening and closing, his third camera-eye. In Holylight, two bureaucrats looked at each other in anger.

"The earthquake has fried that damn robopol's circuits. He has lost track of our man!"

◆

Katryl was the champion of the water games that afternoon. A joyful fever vibrated over the city's red-tinted waterways. Hanging from the round windows of the blue slopes, silver ribbons danced in the wind. As Katryl walked out of the changing room, laughing with his Shuripian friends, a teammate approached Zerune, who was standing on the dock.

"You? On the team, Kol? I pity your team mates!" she said.

"That's because you haven't met our greatest misfortune. Look, this is Katryl. Katryl, meet my cousin, Zerune."

Zerune grinned at Katryl with her eyes as he said "nice to meet you," taking pleasure in the theatrics of acting as strangers.

"Where are you from?" she asked, "Not from Shuripi, right?"

"I was hoping you would've noticed me, since you go to Jos's so often. I know I'm ugly, but…. Where from, you ask? That'd be Holylight."

"Kol, Katryl! You *could* leave girls alone every now and then, you know?" someone said.

Katryl feigned crying when Zerune gave Kol a kiss. Then, he felt it all at once: Zerune's warm kisses on his cheek, an emptiness in his head, the earth rocking under his feet, the splashes of the choppy water, his lover's restless fingers around his wrist, her voice:

"Dear me! Better for it to happen before the water games! This was a 4 on the scale, at least. Are you all right, Katryl? You don't get earthquakes like this in Holylight."

Katryl felt a pang in his heart: the purple open ocean, the small harbor nestled between two rose-colored hills, the houses on their translucent blue stilts, the song of cricket-seaweed rising from the seabed…. The itinerant tavern islands — No. The boy's blue eyes hardened. Self-pity is for idiots, he told himself. He rushed to the hyperlatex kayak, which had the shape of a seahorse, prancing on two fibrous, shaped calves, his body tanned, young and strong. He slipped into the kayak and put on the rowing gloves that went up to his shoulders. He could now hear the languid call of the fragrant and reddish waterways, the challenge of the nimble black boats. And Katryl danced down the slippery paths laid on those waters, catching all the balls made out of floating rock that swayed on roads where no tracks could be left; crouching and bending without ever knocking over his kayak or scratching its hyperlatex, flying until he won.

A fine crease opened on the bald man's forehead, who had shuffled from the basalt bridge down to the Great Waterway quay. Inside the crease, the electronic third eye opened and then made the camera's diaphragm blink in a flash of black light.

◆

Katryl spent the afternoon alone in the tavern. The sky had already gone green. On the streets, Turion's living lights began to cast a soft glow inside their cage-lanterns: it was the yellow fireflies, big as small children's heads. He ran into Lor and Azir and walked with them to their doorstep at the water's edge. There he fed the house firefly some seaweed to hear it sing, a suffocated, unmistakable sound. The water lapped at Katryl's feet in answer to that almost inaudible whistling.

The boy breathed in, feeling the taste of living air, carried by the wind from Holylight's volcanoes, flooding the deepest pockets of his lungs. The laughter of a group of young people reached him over the rumor of the choppy water. He waved at them.

"Hooray for our Katryl! He can swallow the air of the volcanoes without a sneeze, as easily as an old Shuripian!"

The young boy couldn't have known that his cheering had given Katryl away. Katryl, smiling at them, had not noticed the small boat that had stopped in the middle of the waterway, its reactors huffing. He walked back to the tavern alone and, looking back, he recognized the bald man with the vertical crease stealthily hopping from boat to boat. By the time Katryl held his hand to his waist redetonating microneedles were fastened to his head and stomach.

Mik, the telepathic innkeeper, was leaning on one of the building's balconies, savoring the fresh breeze. This is what happened in his mind: a rainbow burned by lightning reflected on the water, stars of pain, the howling of a soul…. It came from nearby. From home. He went swiftly down the stairs, cursing that gift of his that was useless when it came to predicting anything. Down at the inn, the young boys who had cheered for Katryl were looking down at the floor, save for Azir, who was speaking on the videophone. Katryl was lying there, bleeding from the forehead, his sun-blue eyes blinking like an astonished child's, the words "Pat, Pat" constantly coming out of his pallid lips. Nobody knew of any Pat, whether it was a woman, a man, some kind of code or a memory fabricated and inserted by the robopol. By the time they took Katryl, now unconscious, the bald robopol agent was already on board a waterglider bound for Holylight.

◆

The day Zerune went to the hospital, the doctor told her that Katryl had neither woken up nor stirred for the past four days, and that he had had three EEGs that had come out practically flat. In other words, Katryl was done for.

Zerune listened to the typical litany for these cases — "What do you want me to do? We can't just kill him!" — and then, once the doctor was done, barely managing to conceal the hatred in her heart, she replied with a "Thank you, sir," before stepping into the room.

As the medicine man walked away calling her "trash" under his breath, Zerune set eyes on a thin, red-headed nurse, who made for the door and whispered for her to be quiet. The woman showed her an instrument she held in her hand, a sort of test tube with a sharp metallic tip on one end, before putting it into her pocket.

"You're Zerune? It's done!"

Then, she swiftly took her white gown and cap, balled them up, and put them into Zerune's bag.

"I'd better go now. Good thing none of the real nurses saw me! I'll be in the pharmacy, got it?" Zerune nodded. "If you like, Zerune — well, you know. Bye now."

And then Zerune was alone with that strange body stretched out on the bed. Utterly alone. Every now and then she stared at the white line of the thin oxygen tube that clung to Katryl's nose, or looked at Katryl's forehead and black hair, half-hidden under the plastex. A light earthquake (possibly a 3 on the scale) caused the tube to slip out with a tremor soft enough not to stir Katryl. Zerune noticed a grimace of pain that had formed on his blueish lips. The young woman then drew the sheet away, completely uncovering the damaged body pierced by wounds and tubes. Little lights throbbed in the telemonitoring discs on one of his temples, on his chest and stomach, indicating that Katryl was still not suffering any additional internal bleeding or a cardiac arrest. Katryl's chest rose like the tide, but it was mild, too mild, as weak and resonant as Shuripi's waterways.... Zerune caressed his chest. It was hopeless. Katryl was walking alone on a straight, silent, vile path towards his death. Without fear. Without a sigh. Without pain, she hoped.

Zerune felt a silent sob like a knob in her throat. She stood up again. As she coaxed movement back into her limbs, intending to complete her mission with renewed vigor, she grabbed the sheet and covered Katryl's inert young body with the same hand with which she had taken the tubes off. Having lost the urge to kiss the stony face, the young woman stole away like a thief.

◆

The morning Katryl's friends took his body, Shuripi became a blue honeycomb, closed into itself. Windows and doors kept a mourning silence, all the boats slept empty in rows by the docks — all the boats except for those carrying Katryl's dead body, those which followed after it, and the small crimson vessel driven by a sad Zerune towards the Iber waterway.

They poured freezplex on Katryl. The material hardened around him, who now lay within a translucent star, his eyes open and blue as the Turion sun, and thus he was taken towards the border, rocking in the kayak he had paddled in the water games. His brother had come from Holylight, in Basik. His hands were remotely controlling the kayak — now a coffin, adorned with silver ribbons.

In the center of Shuripi, Zerune was approaching door number 18 on the Iber waterway. She slowed down and aimed the boat — whose prow looked a little like an eyebrow — toward the left side of the gate, where she touched the metal plate on the wall with the boat's magnetic anchor. As soon as she looked at the number 18 — the pharmacy — the fear of crossing the threshold gripped her stomach. She thought she heard a hesitating song (Katryl's friends?) coming from afar, hovering over the water and under the big crab adorning the lower archway. Suddenly she ran, leaving behind the pharmacy, where the thin, redheaded woman from the hospital waited for her, and made for the narrow gap by the small door of number 20, crying as she fled through the dark, arched alleyway.

Reaching the fourth level of the tunnel, a spiral stairway sunk in blue-tinted gloom took her to the "meadow," which was in fact the upper part of the hills on which Shuripians carved their homes. Squatting in the white grass, she involuntarily saw what she was trying not to see: far away, in the waterway connecting with the spaceport lagoon, boats like seahorses swimming were accompanying Katryl to the border between Kobol and Basik. The wind did not bring the bitter smell of Holylight's volcanoes, but Shuripi's scent, lodum and salt linden blossom. Alongside the stirring water of the waterways, the warm, sweet breath of her city came to her. As if there had never been a Katryl...

At that instant, Zerune ran out of tears, incapable of linking Katryl's memory to that silent corpse and the boat that carried him. And she remembered what she had come all this way for, realizing that the doubt that had been pressing down on her had dissolved some place between the wind and the canals. She rested there for a long time, gazing at the distant red line that characterized Neobaskia, the border dividing Kobol and Basik. After, she leisurely descended back underground, where the pharmacist lived, held onto the calcite seahorse on the door and knocked twice. The round door turned on its hinges and through it appeared the restless countenance of the redheaded pharmacist. Her name was Begoña.

"Zerune? Come on in."

She was greeted by a group of women who were sitting on the sofas in the living room. One of them stood up.

"Zerune, here already?"

"I didn't go to the funeral," she replied. "You know what I'm here for, don't you?"

"Oh, child! With your eyes still red and all. Come, sit. There, good. Are you sure that this is what you really want, that you are voluntarily asking? We Neobask women only achieved freedom by maintaining the old rites of our ancestors. If you refuse, you will still be one of us.

"I told you yes already! Even if I have to raise the child alone. How do Kep's and Arl's widows manage? Every problem has a solution."

Begoña shook her copper curls.

"Zerune, Arl's wife already had two living children. Kep's was pregnant when he died. Izarne accepted, others refused— but don't forget it will be different with you! The child will not be yours and his. The cell I extracted from Katryl and preserved inside the lancet is a whole cell in itself. If I inoculate you with it, a clone will be created, a copy. In twenty years' time he will look the same as Katryl. If you feel embarrassed, or a little afraid, just say no. We'll give it to somebody else, and that'll be that."

"Embarrassed, of what? Of incest? As if these were the Middle Ages of planet Earth! Leave those Freudian myths to the children. Sisters, the Neobask women have decided so: Katryl deserves to live, both in mind and in flesh. He deserves to be cloned. For the past two centuries we have been cloning the most valuable among our fallen. If one falls, we must create another. Such is Neobask law."

"Very well, then. What will you name him?"

"No. Don't say what you're thinking. He will not be Katryl. Katryl's body, it might be. But he will be a Shuripian by birth. Raised around our waterways, in our caved-in homes, he will be from Kobol by law, but as Neobask as Katryl in spirit. He belongs to the future of our history. Hopefully a happier one."

"And what about you?"

"To me, this clone will be my son. A second opportunity for Katryl and for Neobask people. Thanks to clones, Neobask has six million inhabitants, even when people migrate or fall. Neither Kobol nor Basik will ever kick us out." Zerune smiled unconsciously. "If the men here knew..."

"Don't be silly—they must never find out. They would go mad."

Zerune stood up.

"Enough talk. When will it be ready?"

Begoña walked her to the door.

"Come with me to the lab. I'll get you prepped."

◆

Meanwhile, Katryl's friends reached the end of the waterway, by the sea. There was the lava river that, thanks to the techniques developed by Neobaskian civilization, carried the lava from the ancient volcanoes into the sea. Despite the fact that the official border between Basik and Kobol—the equator—was located five kilometers away, it was here where the Koboldians' domain ended, leaving the river of embers free territory. The lava river was, therefore, officially, Neobaskian territory. So said, after all, an old Neobask song:

*Our land
made of fire
our domain
in flames
our land
water made of fire...*

Katryl's brother pressed a button on the telerudder. The kayak took off from the waters with a splash, flowed down to the reddish dun lava river and began to lazily slide on its surface. Immediately, Azir shot at it with a laser.

This is how it happened: a rainbow made of lightning escaped, drawing a spiral, a slender yellow flame that could have been a human silhouette crouched under the green sky and, finally, everything was mist, a light-blue smoke that rose towards the blue sun and at once sank in the sea.

Then, shuddering from Shuripi to Holylight, shaking the spark of hope that may or may not have been Katryl inside Zerune's womb, the earth shifted in a brief tremor, the spasm after labor, the final contraction.

Three on the Richter scale.

The Exchange

To Krikri

*Never yet have I found
the woman from whom I wanted children,
unless it were this woman whom I love:
for I love you, oh eternity!*

Nietzsche*

Thus Spoke Zarathustra: A Book for All and None, Trans. by Adrian del Caro. Eds. Adrian del Caro and Robert B. Pippin (Cambridge University Press, 2006)

I. ON HOW THE WILL TURNS INTO THE CAMEL

IT WAS FREEZING. In Daleth's thick atmosphere, Wotan had spent that day's afternoon wandering through the planet's rainforests. The heat rose from his lower back all the way to his shoulders, making his feet heavy, lightly shortening his breath. His blue eyes noticed a small, colorful rock standing by a beech. He needed to rest, perhaps slip into dreaming. Wotan's strong shoulders settled against the trunk. His open face tasted the cool air. He was thirsty. He had gotten so far...how far? Toward whom? He remembered. The roads and paths of a host of planets extended inside his mind—rubber trees, flower-doves in thickets, so many women with blue, green, black eyes, their long hands sliding and caressing.... Wotan's heart leapt as if a wound had just opened in it. He remembered his wife, Fricka. Her white-blond curls. Her caresses. Her reproaches: "If only you weren't such a lecher!" He hadn't been unfaithful to her right away—not with another woman, at least. The first time that he had left Fricka, hungry for adventure, he went in search of a machine—planet Baruna's ancient hyperlogitial, the best in all the galaxies—wanting to "acquire" it. Or, rather, steal it.

That was the first time Erda's call reached him. One of the terminals switched on, by itself, and a message appeared on its screen.

The hyperlogitial is harmful to humans.

And under the message appeared a succession of historical equations. Clearly it would be best to leave the hyperlogitial alone! But who had made the call? Wotan used the keyboard to ask: who? Where from?

I'm calling from below the surface of planet Daleth. My name is Erda.

So you can see the future? Wotan asked.

Soon the response appeared on the screen:

Thanks to my mental gifts, I can predict the future; sometimes the past, and, nearly always, the present.

And suddenly the screen went dead.

Wotan returned to Fricka and her berating once again.

"You keep on abandoning your women. I shall raise all of your children. Just to make you feel some shame!"

No sooner said than done: she welcomed eight stepdaughters into Walhall, the satellite palace, all left behind by Wotan. Perhaps she did so because she herself had only given him sons. Wotan saw that wife of his as a lover at times, an adversary at others; but Erda, that mysterious being that kept calling to his terminal, was becoming a friend. A loyal friend who nevertheless called him infrequently, sometimes to give him advice and other times asking for news, as if that was Erda's reward. The conversations did not last long; Erda's answers were always very short. Still, Wotan managed to tease some details out of them.

I can't see.

So Erda was blind. And a living being.

They call me Mother-Memory.

Therefore, a woman.

Finally, one afternoon, Fricka's attacks managed to send her husband into a rage. He in turn attempted his own attack on Erda:

Nobody understands me. Why won't you ever answer me properly?

I can't send long messages through a machine.

Wotan could still hear Fricka's screams in his ears. She was jealous of Erda, too, thinking she was a woman he knew. Why? And, yet — perhaps…

Erda, can't we talk face to face?

On the screen, a series of maps appeared, each more detailed than the previous one: planet Daleth, a continent, a volcano ridge, a field, a little path, three springs, a place where an ash tree stood. And Wotan, spurred by Fricka's jealousy, had flown to Daleth and landed laboriously on that small volcano-ridden planet.

Now his golden body was lying in one of Daleth's forests, asleep under a beech tree.

He startled awake at the touch of something on his face, his hand already around his laser gun. He couldn't see anybody around! What had touched him? Perhaps a bird's wings…. He stood up abruptly. There were no tracks on the ground. A small creature was shaking a blade of grass. A fly? No. But something was slithering on the narrow path. A thin root. No; not a root. A piece of white string. Could it be a trap? Wotan was ready to shoot. On the ground, the white string was stretching out and relaxing back like an elastic band, as if it were tied to something. The string seemed fixed to the earth. Better not touch it!

Where did it "go"? Wotan followed after it — it seemed to lead behind the beech. As he approached the tree, he heard a voice, faint and monotonous.

"Looking ‣ for ‣ Erda?"

Then, Wotan saw it behind the beech tree. It was coming out of the fog, from a row of willows, a sign that there was a river.

It floated. It had no wings, but its feet did not touch the ground. The creature's thin, long legs took steps in the air, as if it were too light for the planet's atmosphere. Its lipless mouth asked again, pronouncing each word separately:

"Looking ‣ for ‣ Erda?"

"Yes."

"Wotan?"

"Yes. Are you Erda?"

"No ‣ Mother ‣ Erda ‣ me ‣ send.
You ‣ leave ‣ must ‣ weapons."

"Wait."

The bald woman reached out and held onto the branch of a young lime tree. Wotan, examining her more closely, had noticed the detail that had led him to believe she was a woman: the being seemed to have breasts. They were, in fact, not breasts, but two mounds of muscle, shaped like pyramids, rising like cymbals every time the creature pronounced a syllable. She must use them for breathing, then. The being was two-legged; her skin was bluish, a turquoise shade. She had normal ears, a baby nose, eyes closed as a blind person's. Wotan's eyes ran over her body: she was wearing a long white jacket. The being was as big as Wotan and had two pairs of extremities. Both arms and legs were slim and looked flexible. The hands were very long, ending in three fingers with no fingernails.

The being was waiting for Wotan, completely still.

"Who are you?" he asked.

"I ▸ Norn 1 ▸ be. Mother ▸ Erda ▸ need ▸ underground ▸ be."

"Is she imprisoned?"

"Erda ▸ no ▸ understand."

"How is she listening to us?"

"I ▸ connected ▸ be ▸ to ▸ Erda. Through ▸ this," said the being, turning her back on him and using one of her bluish bird-like claws to show Wotan a spot under her ear. The white string that he had seen on the ground ended there. Norn 1 took the string in her hand and held it out to Wotan, who took the detector from his belt and held it near it and let out a sigh: no red light, which meant that it was safe to touch. Still, as the man's fingers held the string, he recognized the tickle of a weak electric force and flinched, startled. The string was hot, too. It was alive: he finally understood. It was a nerve, attached to Mother Erda's brain underground.

Within half an hour, Wotan had come to the conclusion that Norn 1, this messenger of Erda's, was able to speak but didn't understand much of what he said. Norn 1 said so herself:

"I ▸ no ▸ understand ▸ all ▸ words. Neither ▸ transmit ▸ to ▸ Erda. You ▸ go ▸ need ▸ to ▸ Erda. You ▸ weapons ▸ leave ▸ here."

Could Wotan trust her? At any rate, she didn't look dangerous, this half-woman creature who didn't know how to use verbs. As if she lived outside of action.

"And Erda will teach me everything I want to know?"

"Yes."

It was clear that the creature knew nothing of sorrow. Wotan quickly put his belt down on the ground, afraid that the blue fingers would touch him. But he made sure not to take off the "handphone," or micro-radio device, that he wore on his wrist. Norn 1 pointed at the way to go. Wotan returned to the path and looked back: Norn 1 was already kneeling on the earth under the beech tree, Wotan's belt and laser gun on her lap, her forehead touching her knees, asleep.

The sun bored through the clouds.

The narrow path ran along the stream. The water was white. In the distance, something white took to the air with a soft sound of wings: Wotan had scared off a swan. At a certain point the path bent away from the stream. In the middle of the bend, Wotan saw Norn 1 sitting among the branches of an ash tree. That made him angry.

"What have I left my weapons to you for, then? What do you want?"

But she wasn't as short-tempered as Wotan.

"You ▸ Wotan ▸ be?"

"You're asking who I am? You don't recognize me?"

"No. You ▸ come ▸ be ▸ from ▸ river ▸ Urd. You ▸ seen ▸ have ▸ my ▸ sister. I ▸ Norn 2 ▸ be."

Then Norn 2 fell silent, as if she were listening to someone. And did Wotan see a tremor in the nerve clinging to her ear? He wasn't sure.

"Mother ▸ Erda ▸ and ▸ you ▸ feel ▸ must ▸ together. You ▸ go ▸ to ▸ the ▸ spring."

Wotan struggled up the path, following Norn 2. A whispering of leaves, water. Was it the spring? At the end of another bend an enormous ash tree appeared. About thirty feet away from it, a spring was flowing with a thin, clear stream of water. Wotan ran to it and drank from it in great gulps, then straightened abruptly as the coldness struck his guts in a terrible wave. His entire body went hard as he quickly became accustomed to the cold. When he returned to the gigantic ash tree, another bald blue head appeared in front of him: another Norn, of course. Norn 1, Norn 2, and now, Norn 3.... It was the first time he looked at one of them from up close. Under the rays of sunlight, her blue skull was as smooth as a baby's. Their closed eyelids looked like gills. No; Wotan could see them better now. Those weren't lids. The skin created the curvature of a lid, but below there was nothing but a fine wrinkle: it could not open; the beings had no eyes. Yet, the three Norns walked with certainty toward Wotan. Perhaps they had a sort of inner radar, in the manner of bats.

"How many of you are there?" Wotan asked.

The third Norn, hanging from a branch with one hand, remained quiet.

"Are you mute?"

Norn 2 spoke as if she had not heard him:

"Erda ▶ reach ▶ shall ▶ you ▶ from ▶ the ▶ ash ▶ tree. Sister ▶ connect ▶ will ▶ you."

Wotan shuddered.

"Connect me? I don't want to be connected."

The other two Norns remained silent and completely still.

Wotan, looking at their strange "breasts," noticed that the Norns only breathed when they spoke.

He'd had enough. He turned his back on them and returned to the trail. The Norns remained still. They didn't care. Further down, in the calm of the forest, he found Norn 1 on her knees, still with his weapons on her lap. As Wotan walked towards her, the guardian stood up and gave him back his belt and gun without a word. As Wotan tied his belt back on, he tried to understand.

"So I can just go?"

The toothless mouth opened slowly, the muscles under the throat slightly rising:

"Yes."

"Erda can't understand me any other way?"

"No."

"And you're not lying?"

A spell of silence.

"Ly-ing? What ▶ lying ▶ be?"

Wotan, a shy smile on his lips, yielded to this being from far away who didn't know what lying was, perhaps because risk had always been his greatest temptation. He slowly bent his strong, golden fingers, slowly untied his belt, and slowly handed it to Norn 1. The webbed hands took the belt without hesitation. Wotan left Norn 1 as before, sitting on her heels with the belt and gun on her thighs and her forehead touching the knees that rested on the grass, and climbed the hill among the silver trunks. His steps were louder this time.

Norn 3 had not left the branches of the big ash tree, still holding on with one hand. Wotan walked straight toward her and confidently took her one empty hand. It felt as cool and smooth as the stem of a plant. Norn 3 little by little intertwined her four-segmented fingers with the man's, then she shook her head, detaching the white nerve that clung to her ear. It fell on Wotan's wrist, heating up and making his arm tingle with a weak electric shock. A pleasant heat spread through Wotan's entire body: Erda's greeting, a kiss of welcome. The nerve's tremor intensified and subsided in turns, but the heat was constant. It couldn't be just a caress. Perhaps it was a code. Norn 2's voice became louder:

"Why ▸ you ▸ respond ▸ no ▸ to ▸ Erda?"

"What did she say to me?"

Where the Norn's eyebrows should have been, a deep V-shaped wrinkle defined her forehead, making the skull look like the back of a beetle. Wotan felt a soft tremor in his arm.

"I ▸ can ▸ no ▸ speak.... You ▸ no ▸ can ▸ understand. Erda ▸ make ▸ do ▸ us ▸ like ▸ you."

Wotan finally guessed the truth: Erda had created the Norns so that she could establish a conversation with him, but she had only used what she knew of humans. Since Erda was blind, the Norns were lacking in many ways. The painful truth hit him like lightning: Erda might be of a different race.

"You ▸ connect ▸ need ▸ to ▸ Erda. Mother ▸ Erda ▸ reach ▸ will ▸ through ▸ ash ▸ tree."

Truly I am something else! Wotan thought. *Leaving a surly but faithful wife behind to come all the way here, the fool, ready to trust a creature I have never seen. Though she has always given me good advice. And, at least, she has let me go freely so far.* A throbbing heat spread through his arm—Erda's call. Norn 2 was propped against the ash, looking at Wotan; she was squeezing a thin root between her feet as if afraid to float away. In Wotan's arm, the trembling heat rose and ebbed with the rhythm of a heart beating. Erda was a friend, but she didn't know humans well, and she could harm him unintentionally. Wotan had to make a decision.

"Norn 2, does Erda know what humans need in order to stay alive?"

The response was immediate.

"Yes ➤ Mother ➤ their ➤ laws ➤ for ➤ life ➤ know."

Wotan, saying nothing, let go of Norn 3's hand and set his back against the ash tree. Nothing happened. Wotan looked around him, spotted Norn 3 on a different branch of the ash tree. Her blue claw-like hands pointed at the sky. Wotan lifted his head, and he saw it—it was silently sliding down. A white nerve, like the ones the Norns had. Yes: Mother Erda came to him through it from the tree. He had to connect to the nerve, but how? Meanwhile, the nerve kept descending gently, ever more gently, toward Wotan. He lifted his arm. The nerve's descent became more attenuated, as if it had lost the strength to go any further. Wotan jumped and held onto a branch with both hands, catching the nerve under one of his palms. It was hot and throbbing, as was Wotan's heart. The white nerve curled around his wrist, touched his sleeve and then became lukewarm and still.

Wotan heard Norn 2's voice.

"My ➤ sister ➤ prepare ➤ shall ➤ you. Then ➤ you ➤ gather ➤ thoughts. And ➤ have ➤ in ➤ mind ➤ you ➤ be ➤ who ➤ how ➤ many. You ➤ where ➤ be ➤ located. What ➤ be ➤ purpose. Erda ➤ read ➤ can ➤ you."

Norn 2 held Wotan's legs up with her extremely long arms. As a faint breeze brushed him, Wotan realized Norn 3 was slowly and calmly taking his clothes off. He shivered under her cold hands. The Norns put his back against the trunk once again as the white nerves tied him to the ash with his hands on different branches.

After a moment, the nerves started growing like ivy, surrounding Wotan's body in a web. He calmed down in the web's heat. Then he remembered he must gather his thoughts. He closed his eyes.

Where to begin? Erda was the first thing that came to his mind. He had spent the last few years constantly imagining what she was like. Was she an old, white-haired woman, standing tall in her body, eyes sparkling? Probably not, being blind. Or was she a young girl with a gifted mind, small breasts on a slim body, hands beautiful and agile, large green-blue eyes on a small face… magnetic green blind eyes shining? Or was she a mother, a fat, black-haired matron? …In any case, he never dared to think that Erda could be ugly. How would he think of her now? His heart saddened. I'm so alone, he thought, and at that, a wave of heat spread immediately through his entire body: a sign that Erda could capture his ruminations.

Even though he was a selfish man, Wotan lacked the capacity to think about himself. Now, however, he had time.

I'm supposed to say who I am—it's easier to imagine who I am to others. Wotan from planet Zeta, Master of the Three Suns. Thanks to our technology, immortal (save by violence). Among the rest of Immortals, the other rulers of Zeta, I hold the title of Great Programmer. For the people of the Sonne system, I'm the lord of the palace satellite named Walhall, its chief. A skilled technologist and coordinator of combat aircraft pilots. A valuable enemy in my Galaxy! To my wife—a bitter smile spread his lips—an attractive, lecherous husband. No: I have never been unfaithful to her, never told her a lie. I have only run away from her, run and returned, and run again, over and over. How many times have I returned to her willingly? I have lied to other women, yes: given them false names and such…. What have I been to them? (Look, I'm speaking as if I were about to die.) According to the mirror, a six-foot tall, elegant, vigorous man, broad shouldered, with a strong and limber golden body, a face well-shaped and proud, piercing blue eyes, and an apparently nice smile.

As for my children—one of the bosses of space! Or perhaps a short-tempered father? They all love each other, in any case…

(Wotan felt an emptiness inside). *What have I given to them? Just their lives. That's all. They aren't like me. They're well reared, well educated…but special, too.*

He remembered. On planet Baruna. Inside the playdome. His daughters doing cartwheels under the big springs, laughing, their arms tanned and slender, their eyes sparkling. He remembered. Hunting in the Kaith forests. The flower-doves flying out of the brambles. Little Thor's bursting laughter. The boy's hands knew already how to prepare the electronic gas-hammer. His red hair shone in the sun as he said "Look, father! My aim is as good as a man's!" Thor's lightning-blue eyes. Thor — his most beloved son.

Wotan came back to his senses: he had left his children a long time ago and was now on planet Daleth, tied to an ash tree by a net of nerves, which spread a weak, hot tremor on him that felt like a caress. As if Erda were seeking to flood away affliction, or as if she wanted to catch another of his thoughts.

*I'm supposed to talk about the way I live…*Wotan thought.

The smell of hot metal on whistling pipes. His throat gagging with the smell of hyperoil. On the small terminal screens, salutes and calls dancing, yellow/blue, yellow/blue. A brand-new engine clinking. A pause. Fear — the first sigh: the aircraft dancing up in the air — up, toward the sky — the stars dancing — up…halfway there…. And GO!

GO! From silent laser cannons, traversing the rainbows…getting lost…. Up and go, my swift hypersteel eagle, my spirited aircraft…. And then the cannons went down! The kiss of the earth: another planet that would have new minerals to offer — metal rivers, new aircrafts, machines half-alive, quickly taking flight….

The terminals' green screens flickering from one message to the next. Bands of questions and answers extending endlessly…. Echoes of shouting. Over! Out! Hello! Help! The constant tremor of the telenews web. The news network always full. The buzzing of the worldcomms…. The web — entangled — Erda.

Wotan woke up to the sensation of something cold on his lips: Norn 3 was giving him water to drink. Among the leaves, a ray of sunlight, orange-colored. Wotan had already forgotten how long he had been tied for. The nerve net was as warm as a blanket, so he did not feel cold. His eyes were shut most of the time, except for when Norn 3 gave him water to drink or sprinkled it on his body. Then, across the path, he could see the second fountain: it was a well, and it seemed very deep, surrounded by a wall of cut black stones. Then he forgot his surroundings again. His mind had weakened by fasting at first, then became sharper. His hunger turned off. Wotan was a quick man; since his body was a tool, solid and precise, a well-oiled machine, he did not easily weaken. Especially since he was still and held in place. He could feel his strength simmering down with an odd kind of pleasure. From reminiscing to dreaming, from dreaming to sleep, he was sliding down the stream as if on a sleek, long boat. He could feel his breath and heartbeats more and more intensely. The air currents of his breath...the breath of the air currents. The wind lightly touched his skin—no, it was Erda's nerves. Inside them, pulse—either from his heart, or from the nerves. The beating went faster at times, slower at others. Wotan could not understand the rhythm of that bubbling heat. What was that strange caressing speech trying to tell him? He already knew that they were the offering of a queen. A decorated glass book—one in a language he didn't speak. In an exact, loving language...Erda was loving, yes. For every time Wotan brought out a painful memory, he noticed a long, gentle caress running on the back of his neck. But how could he respond?

What had he come to Erda for? Why had he become a fearsome, powerful creator of galactic kingdoms? He had done it for his wife and children. And because he sought to reshape worlds and beings. Yes: ambition had taken him to Erda. He had landed on planet Daleth to augment his power. And there he was, hanging from an ash tree. Wotan moved an arm slightly, and he felt something hard on his wrist: the Norn had stripped him, but had left his handphone on, that wondrous intergalactic telephone. The device was his link to his country folk, the machine he wore on his wrist even when he made love, and with which he could call from strange planets. But he couldn't use it with his arms tied. It didn't matter. He fell asleep.

He was suddenly roused by a raven's shrieks. It was dawn. Daleth's star was red still. It looked like a blood orange. Wotan shuddered, his hands prickled by the needles of fear for the first time: he was tied, completely naked, weakened by not eating, and all alone! He could see no ravens in the blue sky, but the shrieking had not stopped. He looked down and felt dizzy. His body felt heavy and was covered in ants. That time, he was glad to see the Norns come! They held him, and he immediately fell into their arms. He didn't feel his body sliding. He realized that Erda had "unlinked" him, left him somehow. He was free.

A timid voice said "I'm cold." It was his own. He was fed up with his voice and body and memories and life. Clumsily, he sat down under the ash tree. Norn 3 brought him his space suit, which he put on with feeble fingers.

Norn 2 approached him with a cup of carved multicolored stone. The drink was unmistakable: it had the sweet smell of shoat's milk. One of the most invigorating drinks in the galaxies. The drink all aircraft pilots carried on board. It was proof that Erda had learned the principles of Wotan's metabolism. Wotan gulped it down, and he soon gained strength. Norn 2 was in front of him, huddled inside a thicket, and seemed ready to talk. Wotan listened intently.

"Erda ➤ learn ➤ do ➤ properties ➤ of ➤ humans ➤ by ➤ touching ➤ you."

Wotan was angry: he had been a thing from which Erda could create a database. Nothing more.

"That was good. Farewell, now."

Full of anger and already standing, ready to go on his way, he heard a serene "Wotan." He sighed and sat back down. Looking at his handphone, he was shocked—he had been suspended for nine days!

"Mother ➤ make ➤ do ➤ us ➤ like ➤ you."

Wotan was irritated:

"What do you mean, like me? You can't walk normally, you don't have eyes —"

Erda said:

"What are eyes for?"

"What do you have in place of eyes?" A moment of silence. Norn 2 looked alert.

"Nerve ＞ nodes."

Nerve nodes? Yes, as if they were plexuses.

"What for?"

"To ＞ be ＞ linked ＞ with ＞ Erda. To ＞ link ＞ you ＞ you ＞ remove ＞ must ＞ one ＞ eye."

At that Wotan was astounded, breathless, terrified, infuriated. Then he came to his senses.

"And then I'll be able to understand her as well as you do?"

"Better ＞ than ＞ us. We ＞ halfway ＞ be. You ＞ full ＞ being ＞ be."

"Are those Erda's words?"

"Yes."

Was Norn 2 telling him the truth? Wotan, distressed, looked her straight in the eyes. *I'm such a fool! She has no eyes.* Then he took the blue bald head between his hands so as to touch the white nerve on the left cheek.

"No lies?"

"Ly-ing? What?

"It's wheAAAH!"

Erda's response shook him down to his bones as violently as a punch. Could it be an oath? Wotan's hands slowly let go of Norn 2's head.

Being a fisherman, where could he run away from the temptation to become a fish? Walhall? Never! So that the Gamma psimathematicians, crouching in their mind-bubbles, or the hermits from Delta could show him the way toward a new aspiration…

No. Wotan wasn't made to live in an underwater cave, nor to be all alone on Delta's green snow. Now he was sure that he had spent all his life talking to himself. The new path would be given to him by the one answering to him. And what Erda had proposed was clear: an exchange.

Why did he decide to do it, in the end? Was it because now his pleasures and joys seemed bittersweet to him, and his missions childish and unimportant? Was he ashamed to return having taken nothing? He did not know. Perhaps he was angry with that beautiful body that had nevertheless brought him no happiness?

"Very well." He cast a sad smile. "Take my eye. I'm ready."

He was already talking to Erda, not the Norns.

"Which one?"

"The left one." Wotan was right-handed.

"Follow!" said Norn 2, and rose in the air. Norn 3 took him by the hand. Wotan felt a shiver as the cold skin touched him.

II. ON HOW THE CAMEL TURNS INTO THE LION or THE SAND MERCHANT

Visita interiora terrae rectificandoque invenies occultum

THE TWO OF them walked up the hill hand in hand, Norn 3 swimming in the air, Wotan huffing and puffing, raising clouds of dust. Through the trees came the song of a water stream. Wotan straddled the brown trunk of a fallen beech and tripped, skidded and was dragged along on his buttocks, as the trail had almost become a hill. Below, in the blue mist, a group of enormous round rocks appeared. An incredibly blue stream flowed and spilled on them. Was it water? It couldn't be. It was too blue. Wotan approached and felt the water's heat: the blue mist was actually smoke.

Norn 3 helped him over the chaos and up to the edge of the water. The stream kept flowing between the rocks, where it lost itself from view. Both halted. Norn 3 disappeared fast as an arrow, but Wotan wasn't so easily shocked. His sharp eyesight soon found the hole in between the great rocks. Norn 3 soon emerged from it, then she sank a multicolored stone cup in the water and handed it to Wotan. He clearly had to drink it. What was that water?

It smelled like grapefruit. Perhaps moved by the dryness of his throat, Wotan emptied the cup. The drink was hot. It had no taste. A heat he knew well fell from his throat to his chest; it felt like ants on his lips. It was as tasteless as water, yes, but it had the effects of alcohol.... Wotan stood at ease in the middle of the warm smoke. He wiped the sweat off his forehead with one hand. He smiled at blind Norn 3. She slowly lowered a slight arm, pointing at the water. Wotan did not hesitate; he undressed and dipped himself into the blue water. There he quickly calmed, admiring the large labradorite crystals (the rocks were as blue as planet Earth). Then

99

Norn 3 reached with a hand and pulled him out. Wotan tottered after that half-flying doll to the hole.

The hole seemed to be the entrance to a cavern, perhaps he could traverse the stream this way. As he entered the cave, Wotan noticed that Norn 3 had already gathered his clothes, deftly folded them and placed them in a corner by the entrance. Those four-boned fingers moved quick as mills! They both stopped. Norn 3 disappeared against the wall. Wotan, as the nerves floated in the air, studied her fingers, searching unsuccessfully for the laser axe that would take his eye. Suddenly, he took off his handphone and threw it onto the pile of clothes. From then on, there would be no messages for him!

A light, cold hand pushed Wotan forward. The cavern was a narrow gallery. Further on, a bluish light—where did it come from?

As they walked, the stream became louder: from the outside, it was a low grumble; inside the cave, it was thunder. The passage widened. The earth became softer and warmer. They walked into a sort of small, circular chamber. Blue light entered from a hole. They were on the other side of the stream. Wotan felt a tingling and looked at the ground: the soil was all white—covered in Erda's nerves. Norn 3—still using only her hands—stopped him. Then, she moved closer and gently ran her hand over his left eyelid. Wotan understood. That was not a mother's or a lover's caress, but a barber's. The time had come. Fear shook him all the way to his sex. On his shoulders, Norn 3's cold hands told him to sit down. Wotan, his heart throbbing, inebriated in the stream's thunder and on what he had drunk, lay down on the hot white earth. He closed his eyes. Something warm slithered up his left check. Suddenly, red lightning. An electric punch to his head. An angry pain in his eye! Wotan trembled violently, dug his fingers into the ground, and soon was calmer, out of breath, in tears. His restless hands slowly opened against Erda's tepid nerves. He remained thus, lying on the ground, as if in the middle of a sandstorm. Red lightning and flames bounced about in his eyes. He no longer felt pain, but his cheek and temple were still swollen and numb. For fear of the pain, he still kept his eyes squeezed shut. It was done. He would now live one-eyed forever; why? In exchange for what?

Then *it* began.

How many times had he been in front of an opposing army, how many times in the midst of a host of enemies? How many times, crestfallen, amidst white lies and defiant silences, had he seen hatred on the verge of crackling in the others' eyes? At such times there were no threats issued — at least, spoken in words — but his enemies' hatred had set his spirit aflame.

It was exactly the same now, but that burning wave in which his soul was drowning was not hatred. It was love. Not human love. Perfect love. Unprecedented. Limitless. Total. It was miraculous.

He felt it on his face, light and warm, like a gentle April breeze. It carried a mother's arms, his first daughter's first smile, a friend's laughter, a lover's lips....

And it was terrible. Because once Erda's mind was inside Wotan's, he could keep nothing from her. Wotan, freed forever from his loneliness, did not know where to flee, where to go. He broke into sobs.

He felt a soft hand stroking his feverish brow. The sigh of the leaves. The light footsteps of his lover approaching, as a sweet voice repeating "I'm with you." Wotan finally recognized those footsteps: it was no lover, but his own heartbeats. The words, however, were not a dream. That quiet, gentle voice he carried inside was Erda's. Wotan tried to answer.

"What do you want to do to me, exactly?"

"To transform you. What is the matter?"

All of a sudden, inadvertently, Wotan relaxed. He wanted peace, and Erda gave it to him at once — the peace he felt sleeping in his wife's arms, the peace of a sunset on a newly conquered planet, of the stars on bluish black nights, the works of Delta's lightning-embroiderers. Erda took all these memories, wove them together, and covered Wotan with them until she blew his secretiveness away to its very last trace.

Wotan saw a watery cave and, in it, a golden man, completely naked, lying on the ground. It was himself. Asleep. In the warm, still waters of peace. He woke up to kisses on his shoulders. It was Erda, kissing him from the inside. He was alone. Outside, whistling — a flute…breath…water. The water from the stream. Wotan slowly came back to himself, to his body. He came to accept this one-eyed body for the first time. On his right was the wall of the cavern. On his left it was forever dark. He turned his head and saw the orifice through which the spring was flowing: a blue light came in through it. He touched his left eyelid with a shy, skittish hand. There was no pain. Under his fingers he felt the dry skin of a shriveled plum. So empty, so barren. There was something further in, but what? Some dirt that had gotten inside it? No. It wasn't a scar either. It was hot, and it vibrated like an energy device: it was a white nerve. It kept him linked to Erda. Linked! He sprang up. Once again inside him bloomed a hot wave; Erda's greeting. Wotan looked around: no Norns. It was better that way. He had to leave all nonsense behind. He was no longer drunk, nor doubtful. Now that he had given up his humanity, he must act like that which he had become, to the end. He must learn!

He walked on down the path. The passage turned into a downward slope. In the distance (was it the end?) he saw a light, orange, or perhaps yellow; could it be sunlight?

It shone in the distance. Farther away than he thought.

The downward slope went on and on.

Wotan's feet felt light.

Erda's nerves were weaving a warm carpet under his feet.

The nerves' soft vibration reached all the way through him.

The slope was becoming brighter and brighter. In his mind, like a bird brooding, he felt a sort of warm, trembling wing. A call. A smile. Mutual attention.

It felt warmer as he carried on, downslope.

His heart was beating.

Light, a beautiful afternoon's light.

In his mind, Wotan felt a band stopping him; a shock of cold ran through his body. He halted on the spot and, gathering his thoughts, understood Erda's message: "Wotan…pay attention. Search around you…search." (Erda did not know how to use the word "look".) Wotan had already forgotten that he was missing one eye, and so he did not notice that on his left the floor of the cave went deeper down. Just as he was about to crack his skull, Erda warned him. Erda, the good friend he carried inside.

Erda, wanting to soothe his fear and remorse, spread a wave of heat through the nerves, which startled Wotan's flesh awake. Wotan was shocked at his desire. *Who* did he desire? He knew that he desired *someone*. How did he know?

As if it all had already happened.

In what time?

But time is not a river. It is a maelstrom. And yet he could not remember what Erda was like. Perhaps she looked like a Norn, but whole, dazzling, hot. Orange colored. Desirable. How could he approach her? Wotan was in a cul-de-sac, after all!

A light blinked. In Wotan's mind, a smooth voice kept repeating "Here I am." Finally, he tilted his head and saw where the light was coming from — a crevice that cave people called a "cat door." It was child's play for Wotan to crawl through it; after his planetary travels, the changes in the atmospheres had given him a dancer's flexibility. His agile, long, and muscled body easily crawled and slipped through. The hardest part was to gather the courage to lift his head. As he did, he stood up and shouted.

"You!"

Wotan felt a peaceful, loving shudder in his body and mind: "Me."

Erda was a bit further below. Wotan stared at her. Erda was sparkling. She was transparent, apricot-colored, and as big as a small room. Was she shapeless? No. She looked like a giant jellyfish, or a mushroom. The white nerves slid through the ground and into the gelatinous flesh, forming sharp star-like ends — plexuses. That being was not built for movement, that was clear! No legs, no eyes, no brain — but each knot of nerves, each plexus, could do an entire brain's job, and each nerve could extract nourishment from the plants outside. It was a maze of memories and thoughts. No arms, no sex, no heart, and yet a soft, hot wave kept lunging at him, as the smooth voice repeated "What do you want?" in his mind.

And perhaps because there was no other way he could respond, Wotan, his body on fire, descended and took shelter, pressing himself against the heavy, gelatinous sea of flesh. The hot skin, smooth as an apricot, moved under his lips. Inadvertently, Wotan opened his arms in an embrace. The last sound he heard was her voice: a lament? A call? Everything rolled and poured, and Wotan violently sank into pleasure.

III. ON HOW THE LION TURNS INTO A CHILD

WOTAN FELT LIGHT, blissful, and exhausted. Lazily he opened his arms. Feeling kisses on his lids and sides, he opened an eye — it was night. He bitterly remembered it was the empty socket and wanted to scream...but couldn't. The taste of plums filled his mouth. He wanted to open his other eye: vainly. He stiffened with fear. The wave of a caress enveloped him. Finally, he opened his eye, shook his head and, as he tried to move, spun on himself. He was underwater, in warm, apricot-colored water. Breathless! Was he dying? No: he was fine. The water was full of stars. Had Erda swallowed him? Once again the wave of a caress led him to pleasure. When he awoke, his worries had gone away, for he knew that she could feed him. And she could give him oxygen too.

"Let's talk now" said the quiet gentle voice inside him. Wotan opened his mind to Erda, as he kept swimming inside her — inside that maze of memories and thoughts...

What planet are they on? They are slowly flowing along the branches of an octopus-tree. They whistle forward. They look like resin, or slime. As green and bright as glowworms. All of that tree's metallic sweat has burned away — lightning. They are no longer resin; they are sparks, dispersing into space by millions! At least a million sparks. Are they conscious? Now they are flying from asteroid to asteroid. They will lose vigor, or energy, and fall back to earth to become resin again, to again flow in search of metals.

Wotan keeps swimming in the maze of Erda's memories...

☙

The sea, under the green sky, is blue. The sand on the shore is rose-colored, warm, smooth as velvet. A copse of "trees" with no trunks. Latex-like branches forming bridges and tangles. Most times they are squatting, since they can endure neither sun nor clothing. However, if you ardently wish them to, they will remain with you under the sun, talking, until they die. For life matters nothing to the plant people. Friendship, on the other hand, is the only value they hold.

Some are green, others are lily red. They all have sparkling skin. Their hair is either green or champagne. They look at you with wide green eyes, smiling. The plant people are always small, slim, and tender. Their gestures are a dance. Your eyes look away uncomfortably from the women's small, firm breasts, for you are disturbed by their stillness. The plant people do not breathe. The gas they need they take through their skin. They are mute and telepathic. Over in a corner there are two small, green children, perhaps brother and sister. They meet your gaze and soon come toward you. Their voices are already in your head: "We're tele-paths, yes — don't be afraid! We only do it if you want us to. Did you really think that we telepaths can force our way into others' minds?" The little girl's green eyes turn thoughtful. If Wotan had a daughter — if she were a telepath…. The girl smiles: "You can't become a telepath. But just by studying other people's gestures and small movements, you can guess a great deal! For example…"

Her long green hands move like leaves in the air, dancing, bending, floating, whirling. Wotan learns, wishing to drown in the peace of those green eyes. In the sea of her eyes. Green… eyes…gre…Er…da.

☙

"Erda, I'm still inside you! What were those planets?"

"I have found them in a memory of mine."

"But how can you show them to me, being blind?"

"I'm not blind. The vibrations that you perceive with your eyes, I perceive in a different way. Also from afar."

"You can see wherever you want?"

"And whenever, too."

♋

Wotan keeps swimming in the maze of Erda's memories…

♋

The smell of molten metal in the air. Where? To the left, a demolished palace, vitrified by fire, which Wotan quickly recognizes: the Black Palace of Baruna. Oh, yes. It's true. For the past three years, he has been warring on planet Baruna. In the mist and freeze. He cannot believe that this frozen desert used to be Baruna. Sonne, the sun, is now fat and red: it is constantly growing colder. An old sun. Whatever damage not caused by Sonne's aging, the lasers and hypernitros of king Fenrir's army has. The earth of planet Baruna, slit open by microseisms, pierced by meteorites, now looks like a wound. First, the sea coast drowned at many points under the pounding of the waves. And Fenrir, Wotan's foe, always hungers to take Baruna. Wotan knows he is in the middle of this war, but when? Later, too late…. Too in the future.

The air is filled with explosions and yellowish smoke. Wotan walks and walks amid the laser rifles' rainbows. Next to him is a hulking, red-bearded man: Thor, his beautiful son, is raising his arm—he holds his electronic gas hammer in his hand, ready to sear the enemies' eyes and tetanize their bodies.

"Father, watch out!"

A black cloud of ash is floating towards Wotan. It's Fenrir's famous wolfpotamuses! They have pillars of steam instead of legs. Thor shouts. Wotan trips and falls. From the ground, he sees one of the wolfpotamuses approaching. The machine's head opens— Wotan turns and crawls—he must roll over. If not, he will be absorbed into a wolfpotamus's mouth and disintegrated within it—or frozen, if Fenrir wants him alive. Wotan keeps scrambling. He scrambles…scram…bles…Erda.

♋

Wotan is inside a warm wave. The wave is the color of apricots.

"Erda, what did you show to me? Is it the future? Is it my death?" But Erda has already taken him to pleasure.

♋

Wotan keeps swimming in the maze of Erda's memories...

♋

Night time. In the forests of Baruna, the small moons barely cast their lights on the fir trees. Wotan, in the dark, is hidden, with pleasure. Waiting.

A crack. Among the branches, two yellow stars are approaching. Two yellow eyes, sparkling, dilated — a wolfwoman. Wotan is glad. Under the midnight white moons, in a clearing, he sees the wolfpeople's dance, a small ring of frenzy. The girls' hair flowing in the wind. One of them looks at Wotan. Her long ears are pure white under the full moons.

Dawn. In the sunrise's white mist, Wotan's steps trip over and over on the black trail. A child's laughter. Two children's. A double laughter. Wotan walks down the trail. He is not alone. In his hands he holds the soft, chubby warm hands of two children — his son and daughter: four blue eyes, a single twin gaze. The boy and girl have Wotan's eyes. One...eye.... Blue eyes and laughter in the center...eyes...in center...in Erda.

♋

"Erda — for an instant I thought I was outside."
"You don't remember?"
"What?"
"That this will happen to you one day?"

♋

Wotan keeps swimming in the maze of Erda's memories...

♋

The black-haired slender girl has eyes that look askance at him. Gray. Sparkling. Like quicksilver. Dark and full. Her face is fine; her shoulders, strong; firm breasts and lips. Her fingernails are white. She does not smile in your arms, for Theta-Centaurians do not know about feelings. She is free of love, hate, and envy. Forever. That may be the reason why her race has so exhaustively researched the syndrome of pleasure/pain, to the point of becoming masters in this science.

The man (where is he from? Human, in any case) has been brought to the girl. When they put him down on the bed, he was lamenting. Now he is still, but his jaw is tense, unable to overcome his stiffness. His body is covered in wounds and bruises, he has been injured in an accident, or perhaps in a fight, he looks as if he has taken a beating.

The girl's fingers softly touch some points of his body. What is so special about those points? For they are not nerve nodes, nor places where organs are located. It seems that the girl wants to feel certain echoes. She gently touches the wounded man, and soon he calms down. People on planet Theta have long forgotten about mental illnesses, too; they need apothecaries and barbers, but not physicians.

The glass on the window is apricot colored. Wotan rests his forehead against it. He feels a kiss on his shoulder—his mouth is filled with the sweetness of plums. No—it is not glass.

♋

Wotan somersaults in Erda's waters; he shudders. He is so cold! Erda's voice is in his mind:

"Wotan—you want a woman."

"Erda…what am I to you? A lover, or someone to give you a child?"

Erda answered with another question.

"Wotan—do you want a child, or not?"

And Wotan, shocked, felt the need to admit the truth to Erda and to himself. Yes, for the first time, he wanted a child. The others (three sons and eight illegitimate daughters) he had made by accident. He was glad when they were born, proud when they matured, but when they grew separate from him in opinion or feeling, he always felt sad. Yes, he desired a child. But Erda's child.

Such a dream. That Erda monster gave him sexual pleasure, that was certain, but how would she give birth to a child?

"It's easy, Wotan."

Easy! A silent burst of laughter shook his belly.

"Well, Wotan—this is what you want: a being just like you, but with two eyes and the gift to think a little within my memories. Do you not?"

"Yyyes."

"Very well, then. I shall make a clone of you, but with an improved brain."

"You…what?"

"I said, I will clone you. I will copy you out of one of your cells. I will give you a son that will be your double."

Wotan felt himself going mad: another son, a second Wotan, one that would become a man and face him as himself…. Certainly not! He choked in fear. He was sick of himself.

"No, Erda, not that! And besides, I'd rather have a daughter."

"Fine. I will make her out of your seed, then."

Wotan, thinking that the other half of the cell would belong to Erda, felt frightened again, imagining a half woman, half gelatin monster. Afterwards, thinking of the Norns, he felt ashamed. Those three, linked to their mother by a chain of nerves; servants without a mind of their own. Not that!

Nevertheless, at that moment, he understood that what Erda had done to the Norns he himself had tried to do to his children, if in a different way. He felt a mental caress.

"No, Wotan. Do not fear. Our daughter will be a beautiful woman. Blue-eyed—yours."

"No, not mine! She must be free!"

Wotan had never wished freedom on a child. But he had accomplished and learned so much on his way to Erda. A loving wave threw him down a chasm of pleasure.

A mild pain soon woke him up. It was as if something was pulling at his sex and his left eyelid. All around him, Erda went red and almost contracted. The sweetness of plums in Wotan's mouth became increasingly intense. In his mind, a comprehensible message: Wotan was feeling Erda's pleasure for the first time. As if that pleasure she felt came from Wotan's request for freedom for his child, Erda was giving birth with delight. And she rocked him from dream to pleasure, from pleasure to memories or reveries of the future, for a long time, until he forgot where, when, who he was.

♋

He woke up in an apricot-colored sunrise. Again that plum sweetness in his mouth, a tingling in his left eye socket. Tilting his head, he saw something rolling around inside the gelatin, which was linked to him through an eye. Up, Wotan kept inadvertently shifting in and out of sleep, swimming in the maelstrom of time, until a new voice appeared inside his mind.

The voice was pure as crystal. Cheerful as a glockenspiel or a set of bells, clinking. All questions, all smiles. Wotan felt as if a bird's heart were beating against his. A bird's light heart, impossibly soft under warm feathers. He was raising a child for the first time — or was it the other way around? He entered a magnificent happiness. The minds of father and daughter kept wandering and getting lost in the maze of Erda's memories. They invented myriad games, such as:

> Guessing which was the largest planet
> the hottest planet
> the most docile, the fattest, the bluest beast…
> the most melodious tree…

Through Erda's intangible memory passages they raced, the three of them, stealing yesterday's and tomorrow's memories from each other. Wotan had a companion, a gifted daughter whom in Erda's waters he could hardly see and never embrace. Sometimes he saw her eyes — blue as the sky. Wotan's eyes.

♋

Wotan keeps swimming in the maze of Erda's memories…

♋

That looks like a rock. What world is he in? From up close, it could be a piece of pyromorphite, or a sponge. But that is not a rock nor a sponge. It is alive. It swells and empties itself; the shocks of green on it—could it be skin?—turn yellow and back to green, following a rhythm: green/yellow, green/yellow, green/yellow.... Inside Wotan, Erda's gentle voice: "This rhythm is a formula model, Wotan. It is the thought pattern of any living thing anywhere. It is immutable, the same in all places. And it is the base of an intergalactic code. Even if your interlocutor looks like a sponge or a wolf, you can understand them through it."

"..."

"Wotan—you don't understand?"

A pause. Wotan felt a tingle on the back of his head. The gentle voice spoke again:

"Ah, yes. Your brain can't do it. There are many things you can learn, however. For example—"

And Wotan learned.

♋

The child is innocence and forgetting,
a new beginning, a game...
a first movement,
a sacred yes-saying.

Nietzsche

♋

And that which was bound to happen finally happened one day. Through one of Erda's memories, Wotan and his daughter learned about a distant planet. Most of its inhabitants looked like goat people, or satyrs; when they danced, they made music with their crystal toes. The little girl tried to do the same thing, in vain. She called for Wotan.

"But I have feet!"

"Yes, my love, but that planet is outside."

"What is outside?"

Wotan's mind darkened. He also could not deny that watching those dancers had made him want to move, himself. Erda carefully, intensely caressed him, and little by little he slid from pleasure into sleep.

♋

Wotan woke up outside.

His socket hurt a little. He was lying on the cave floor. Next to him, against Erda's gelatinous mass, was a sleeping little girl, her small, chubby hands clinging to Erda. Wotan's heart skipped: that was his daughter, and she was at least four years old! Had they been inside of Erda for that long? He was afraid to look at his face in the mirror. Squinting, he touched his left eyelid with a finger. There was no nerve; his link to Erda was gone. One-eyed, alone, and free…

He walked back to where his daughter was and bent down. He was mesmerized. The child's breath was like pure, fresh air to him. Her cool lips seemed rose leaves. Wotan stroked her blond, curly hair and kissed her silky cheek until she woke up. She opened two blue eyes, which widened and then welled up. The girl started to sob — she was no longer linked to her father's mind. When two small arms circled his neck, Wotan too began to cry. Having been the matrix to which his child was tied, what must he become now? Wotan taught his daughter her name for the first time, using words and gestures.

"You, Brünhilde."

The little girl, hearing the sound of a voice, smiled and sought shelter against her father's body. Then, she softly patted Wotan's chest with a small hand. Wotan read the question in her blue eyes and taught Brünhilde her second word:

"Father."

Wotan turned his back to Erda, not daring to look at her, and made for the passage with his daughter in his arms. In those last four years, the cat door had become a natural doorway (or Erda had made it into one). Forgotten sensations came back to

Wotan one by one: how strange, the weight of that body made of flesh and bones! The swelling and emptying of their chests, their breathing stoking echoes in the passage, the child's warm head against his shoulder...

In the middle of the corridor, the three Norns gave Wotan his clothes and Brünhilde a white coat, and brought them some apples and a mug of shoat's milk for each. Wotan relaxed when he saw his daughter gulping the milk down.

They needed to get out of the cave. To Wotan, it felt like the sorrow and fear following a new birth. Once again he had to choose to be human. He was dazzled by the star Sonne. Brünhilde curled up like a kitten and reached for the sun, which was surprising, since Wotan had not yet put her down from his arms. The child chirped as she pulled at her father's beard; the father smiled. In their eyes, so alike, color sang; the sun was so red, the leaves so green, the sky so blue. The arms of the trees danced and danced. Brünhilde could not help smiling even when Wotan tripped on the path; his fearless daughter filled him with pride.

Wotan stopped by the stream and set Brünhilde on the grass. The child almost fell, then walked on all fours and soon was already running around like it was nothing, delighted at this new game. Her father watched her gallop. Brünhilde learned to hop and sprint as easily as a goat. Three hours later, father and daughter, racing each other, throwing all seriousness into every black hole in the Galaxies, threw themselves onto the grass.

EPILOGUE

NIGHT TIME. IN the forests of Baruna, the small moons barely cast their lights on the fir trees. Wotan, in the dark, is hidden, with pleasure. Waiting.

A crack. Among the branches, two yellow stars are approaching. Two yellow eyes, sparkling, dilated — a wolfwoman's. Signy's. Wotan is glad. Signy is already in his arms. She is smiling, as Wotan has tried in vain to hide, for wolfpeople can see in the dark, and from afar, too. Wotan grabs Signy by the waist and takes her to a new wooden cabin. Signy is amazed.

"Who built it?"

"I did. For us."

It is done. Signy will leave her people and live with Wotan. The two of them enter the cabin.

"Hold on," says the girl, putting the small bag that she carried on her shoulder on the table and taking a piece of fruit from it. Smiling sweetly, she feeds Wotan the fruit. Wotan's heart pounds, recognizing Erda's plum flavor. Is he ashamed, sad, or hopeful? He does not immediately dare to touch Signy; he sits her down on the chair by the hearth. The fire lights up the wolf girl's golden eyes. Small and sharp bluish teeth glint on a dark face. She keeps repeating that she wants to live with Wotan forever, and Wotan, answering fondly, thinks of the twins he saw in Erda's memory. He knows they will be born from Signy's womb. He distractedly caresses the girl's wavy hair. Signy's mouth seeks Wotan's…

No — time is not a maelstrom. It is a pool.

♋

It is light already; Wotan is awakened by the sound of wings. Crowtel and Blackhole, the tame crows that he brought from Daleth, fly into the room and stand in a corner. Signy, beside

Wotan, still sleeps in the fur-covered bed. Wotan gets up slowly, gazing at his beloved. He remembers last night's movements to the point of madness, especially thinking how she touched his two eyes and cheeks. As if he still had two healthy eyes.

He also remembers his wife Fricka's gesture. That gesture that made him run away to planet Baruna, to this wolf people's primitive civilization, to Signy. Because of that gesture, Wotan has left his beloved daughter Brünhilde to Fricka—to Fricka and to Erda, for she is telepathically linked to her mother. Wotan could not bring her away from Walhall's satellite palace. She is Wotan's daughter, and she must learn about the techniques of an advanced civilization. Yes: the Master of the Three Suns' daughter had to stay. But the father had to leave.

Wotan remembers Fricka's gesture. It happened the day he returned to Walhall. Upon arrival at the palace, Wotan found out through the radio that his sons were waiting for him at the space-port. As he landed, instead of two boys he found two men: four years had passed. Both quick and beautiful. He recognized Thor by his red hair; Baldur, by his sweet smile. Vidar had stayed with his mother; that one had always taken her side, had always gone against his father. Brünhilde came out of the aircraft, and Thor's expression darkened. Baldur crouched and opened his arms to the child. The little girl confidently ran to him, and both of them headed to the palace, hand in hand. Thor walked with his father, after the others, in silence.

Wotan met his wife in the palace. Vidar stood next to her.

"Father brought you another sister," Thor said to Vidar, avoiding looking at his mother. Wotan felt it like a slap. Thor! His very own Thor thought Brünhilde was just like the rest of his daughters! And the truth dawned on him like a lightning of pain: the others, unlike him, did not know what it was like to listen empathically to one another.

Baldur embraced little Brünhilde and took her away from the room. The rest walked out soon after, to leave Wotan and Fricka alone. Fricka started with her attacks; Wotan kept silent. Suddenly, by chance, Fricka looked Wotan in the eye. She turned pale.

After a long silence, Fricka made the gesture that Wotan would never forgive her for: she caressed the eyelid of his empty socket with her hand. Wotan would not accept pity. Still, if Fricka had said nothing, if she had acted as if she had seen nothing, perhaps he could have let it go. And he did try to forget. Both the gesture and the question he tried to forget in Fricka's arms; and he succeeded — until dawn, at least.

At sunrise, he awoke. And he remembered. Then he left without saying goodbye, returned to his aircraft and took to the sky, for not even pleasure had managed to banish the question that kept running in his mind.

No, it would not go away.

For when Fricka had asked him "What happened to you?", a world of wonder had blown to pieces within Wotan. From then on he was no longer able to lie to himself. At that moment he had understood that he had been a fool to return from Erda straight to Fricka. Now he had certainly been unfaithful to his wife. Not by leaving her side, but by returning to her!

How could he tell her what had happened? What could he say? Once again he was forced to return to words humans used to listen to one another, to not listen to one another, full of interferences, of words stopped mid-sentence, mid-thought! He had forgotten the lies humans told when they spoke. What had happened, how could he express it?

Fricka, more hastily, but resolute, asked again:

"Wotan — what happened to you?"

He had to give her an answer. So he said:

"An accident!"

Afterword:
The Life and Work of Mayi Pelot, A Trailblazer of Basque Science Fiction

Oihana Andión Martínez

THE STORIES IN this book may not look different from other science fiction you have read: futuristic technology, environmental disasters, life on new planets, androids killing humans, love, and wars. All of these elements are present in Mayi Pelot's work. The X factor, in this case, lies predominantly with the author's background and national identity.

Mayi Pelot was, in a way, a product of speculative fiction herself; a writer from the future. And not because she believed herself to belong to a world of her own creation, not at all, but because she was ahead of her time on the stage of Basque literature. She was the first Basque writer to immerse herself in, write, and publish science fiction consciously, as a genre. Her background in literature and Greek and classic mythology, as well as her love for science fiction authors like Ray Bradbury, heavily influenced her writing, making it intricate, intertextual, and poetic.

After she stopped publishing in the mid-1990s, it took decades before the genre re-emerged in the Basque literary arena, and by then Pelot had become the primary reference of Basque science fiction. Basque writer Iban Zaldua, who has cultivated the genre himself, mentions her as the only woman among the "specialists" of the genre to emerge in Basque literature in the 1980s and '90s.

Since Mayi Pelot's stories will be new to most Anglophone readers, what follows is meant to provide some context by discussing the Basque nation, the decade of the 1980s, Basque literature, and, of course, the life and work of Mayi Pelot.

EUSKAL HERRIA

(The Basque Country; Euskal = Basque, Herria = People/Land)

The Basque Country is a stateless nation of over 3 million people, split between Spain and France, with the Pyrenees as a natural border. The land on the Spanish side is formed by four provinces and known as the Southern Basque Country (SBC) or "Hegoalde"; the land on the French side, on the other hand, has three provinces and is known as the Northern Basque Country (NBC) or "Iparralde." Spanish is the main language of the SBC, and French is the main language of the NBC. Basque is spoken throughout the entire territory but in much lower numbers; also, 99% of Basque speakers are bilingual in Spanish or French.

After the French Revolution in 1789, France established French as the only official language of the country; the many other languages that existed in the land were not promoted or funded by the government. These restrictive measures resulted in a sharp decline in the number of speakers of Basque and other languages such as Breton or Occitan. In 1936, Spain suffered a three-year civil war as result of a coup led by fascist Francisco Franco. His victory was followed by a dictatorship in which he held power for 40 years. While the prohibition of Basque can be traced as far back as the 13th century, when the crown of Aragon banned Basque alongside Arabic and Hebrew in the town of Huesca's market, it intensified in the 17th century, when the use of Basque was prohibited in schools and bookkeeping. In the 20th century, Franco embarked on a mission to obliterate it completely. During his dictatorship, all languages and dialects other than Spanish were banned in public spaces, striking a big blow against the viability of the already ailing Basque language; cultural production in Basque was condemned to underground movements or to the Basque diaspora spread across Europe and America.

Starting in 1964 and going through 1968, a group of Basque intellectuals gathered to establish the foundation of a unified version of Basque that would allow all future generations of Basques from NBC and SBC to use their language outside of their towns and everyday life. It was meant to be a tool to be used with family and friends but also for administrative purposes, science, education, academia, and literature.

After Franco's death in 1975, a transitional period toward a democratic government followed in Spain and the SBC. Basque had official status for the first time, and cultural production boomed with new books, literary magazines, audiovisual content, and radio shows. Adults who were not able to learn the language in their childhood did so now through the Basque alphabetization programs available across the land.

In 1981, around the same time Mayi Pelot began publishing her work, François Mitterrand rose to power as the first socialist president of the Fifth Republic of France. There was a definite turn to the left: Mitterrand's government nationalized financial institutions, abolished the death penalty, and provided more funding to cultural and social programs. On a darker note, the 1980s was one of the bloodiest decades in the so-called "Basque conflict." ETA (Euskadi Ta Askatasuna), an armed nationalist and separatist organization for the independence of the Basque Country, planted bombs, and kidnapped and shot politicians, businesspeople, and regular civilians as a political strategy against the Spanish and French governments. In response to such violence, both governments inflicted powerful oppressive measures on the Basque population, resulting in deaths and trauma across the territory.

The radical Basque nationalist movement garnered so much political and media attention that other social causes, such as LGBTQI+ rights or the environment, began to have a secondary role in agendas for social change. Their interpretations of a more just and egalitarian society were tinged with nationalist influence, whose struggle par excellence was the sovereignty of the Basque Country.

In this context, science fiction allowed Mayi Pelot to escape a limited understanding of what the Basque Country could become. In her speculative fictions, Pelot offers a subaltern perspective of the Basque experience. By extracting the Basque Country from her contemporary context, she invites the reader to reconsider the concept of nation, the role of women in society, and the threat that globalization and environmental pollution poses to our societies. In her interview with authors Itxaro Borda and Josu Landa, Pelot explains that by providing the reader with multiple future scenarios, one can raise awareness about real problems in the present (Borda & Landa, 1986).[1] In *Memories of Tomorrow*, she warns us of the dangers of nuclear conflict, gentrification, and the oppression of the Basque Country by new, more powerful countries and multinational companies.

Nuclear energy is an important subject in Pelot's work. In "The Digital Maze," we learn that the SBC was decimated by a nuclear explosion during WWIII. The story seems to have been inspired by the concerns surrounding a nuclear plant that was projected to be built in Lemoiz, a town close to Bilbao, the biggest city of the Basque Country. Building work began in 1972, while Franco was still alive. During the Transition years, the news media revealed that planning and construction had begun without the informed consent of the locals, and that the construction company had operated without a license, among other safety violations. Environmental organizations were beside themselves, raising concerns about potential leaks and radioactive waste. Anti-nuclear organizations formed in every neighborhood; protests were frequent and grew larger, until a sizable minority of the Basque society was against the activation of the plant. The relevance of the matter attracted the attention of ETA, which physically attacked the plant and the construction company a few times and took the lives of several people, including workers from the plant, its chief engi-

---

1   This is my own translation. All translations in this article are my own unless otherwise stated.

neer, and his successor. In 1984, following the Spanish general election, the governing PSOE party issued a moratorium on new nuclear power plants in the country, finally putting an end to a project that was already long paralyzed by social and environmentalist pressures. Identified at the time as a real threat to the well-being of Basque society, a successfully constructed Lemoiz plays a central role in Mayi's imagined future.

BASQUE LITERATURE AND THE MAIATZ PUBLISHING HOUSE

Literature in the Basque regions is mostly written in French or Spanish, the prestigious languages, and that is because even centuries before the French Revolution or the prohibitions of Francoism, Basque was considered a second-rate language, relegated to the private sphere of the house and the family. Most of monolingual and bilingual Basque speakers did not know how to write in Basque, even in the 20th century. One of the reasons for this is that, until the end of the 20th century, it did not have official status. The languages of the public, academic, religious, and legal spheres have been the official ones: Spanish, French, and Latin. These languages were imposed at an institutional level, taught in school, and expected to be used in public relations. The written or oral use of official languages endowed the user with a higher social status.

But that does not mean that literature in Basque does not exist; Basque stories have been transmitted orally. In fact, oral literature in Basque is rich and varied. Basque mythology and centuries of Basque history have been collected in tales, sayings, couplets, verses, and ballads. One of the most idiosyncratic forms of Basque oral tradition is *bertsolaritza*, or improvised verse, a community activity in which singers improvise verses on current issues. This practice was traditionally masculine, but, recently, more women have engaged in *bertsolaritza*, breaking barriers and renewing the field. Today, it enjoys a great deal of popularity.

Because the number of texts written in Basque prior to the 20th century was minimal, any such document, fiction or non-fiction, has been recognized under the umbrella of Basque literature. In the 16th, 17th, and 18th centuries, texts published in Basque focused mainly on Basque linguistics and religion. The written literature that is published from the end of the 19th century to the mid-20th century has nationalist and traditional overtones. They extol Catholicism, tradition, and rural and agricultural life in contrast with the hybridity of Basque urban environments, to which many Spaniards were migrating to find a job in the emerging industrial sector. Basque nationalism intended to define the Basque race and its purity. A pure Basque woman, for instance, should be a patriot, take care of her family, aspire to be a good mother, teach Basque values and tradition to her offspring, and live a quiet life in the home environment.

In the second half of the 20th century, Basque literature became more self-aware and moved away from the *costumbrista* style to explore existential issues. The writers of that time read and translated authors such as Franz Kafka and Albert Camus. In their texts, they speak of death, loneliness, and failure. With the unification of the Basque language in the late '60s came a boom of writers. Some authors of this era learned Basque as adults, and many of them were university students who lived in the city. The literature of that era is social, observing and analyzing the problems that afflict society. Bernardo Atxaga, the most international author of Basque literature thanks to *Obabakoak*, began to make a name for himself because he completely broke with nationalist ideas and immersed himself in experimentation with language and new, European ideas. In the literature of the 1980s, the predominant settings of Basque stories shifted from rural to urban areas, and authors played with forms of magical realism and surrealism imported from foreign literatures, broke with the binarism of nationalism, and allowed introspection. They felt a need to redefine themselves as individuals and as a community.

Most of the women writers who emerged from the '80s reflect on women's bodies, motherhood, and the role of Basque women in the Basque socio-political situation. The novels *Koaderno gorria* (*The Red Notebook*) by Arantxa Urretabizkaia and *Bai... baina ez* (*Yes... But no*) by Laura Mintegi talk about women largely in women's voices, although their female characters still fill patriarchal archetypes (virgin, mother, whore). Itxaro Borda and her work are also worth mentioning. Borda is Basque-French, and she and her friend Mayi Pelot were two of the founders of the Maiatz publishing house, which would be home to all of Pelot's work. Borda's most popular character is detective Amaia Ezpeldoi, the protagonist of a crime fiction series spanning six volumes, the latest one of which was published this year. Ezpeldoi is an alter ego of the author: both the author and the character are queer and very interested in discovering the secrets hiding in the depths of the Basque Country and Basque identity. Borda's multifaceted work has received considerable critical attention and is highly regarded for its hybrid approach to Basqueness. Her work, together with the work of other women writers of the 1970s and '80s, represent a before and after in literature written in Basque. Their work laid the groundwork for future women writers wishing to give voice to their own Basque experience.

Mayi Pelot's work contains many of the characteristics present in Basque literature of the '80s, including the view of literature as a tool for social commentary, the experimentation with language, the influence of foreign literatures, a reflection on Basque history and identity, and the introduction of female leading voices.

The Basque Country of the 1980s was influenced by the ideals of the punk movement that burst on the scene with great force in response to the years of repression and censorship by the Spanish dictatorship. Basques were curious about other ways of living and seeing life and were calling for full freedom of expression. It was a time for experimentation in the arts and culture, which was reflected in the texts of Basque writers and in the publishers that sponsored them, especially in *Maiatz*, a literary magazine in the NBC founded in 1982, which two years later became a publishing house, too. Both the magazine and the publishing house were born with the intention of breaking away from the traditionalist

editorial lines of the time. It provided a space to think and speculate about new worlds and political ideas; it was inclusive of all
genres, styles, approaches, and foreign languages and writers
through translations and adaptations. *Maiatz* was a launch-pad
for Northern Basque writers. At the time, and still today, the NBC
was at the margins of Basque cultural production. With *Maiatz*,
writers had the chance to experiment with their language and to
explore at length the relevant matters of the North.

Mayi Pelot, a Basque woman from the NBC who wrote sci-
ence fiction, is a rarity. If it hadn't been for *Maiatz*, she would have
found it difficult to publish her work; the Basque literary system
is predominantly male and focused on authors of the SBC. And
through *Maiatz* she found a group of like-minded people who
also challenged traditional Basque identities and the marginality
of their region in relation to the SBC, and who had questions and
hypothetical answers about the future. And in science fiction, she
found the perfect laboratory for inventing new Basque Countries,
at a time when the nationalist movement monopolized the imagi-
nations of Basque people.

BASQUE SCIENCE FICTION

Science fiction, although increasingly popular, is not a main-
stream literary genre. Add a minority language to the mix, and it
is unsurprising that science fiction in Basque has not been a par-
ticularly fruitful genre. Jose Luis Alvarez Enparantza Txillardegi
made a very brief foray into science fiction with his short story
"Kosmodromo," written in 1969 but published in 1984. Really, it
was a political commentary disguised as science fiction. He wrote
the story just after Neil Armstrong reached the Moon, and, as the
author himself describes in the preface of his book, he wanted
to warn against the naive optimism that had spread throughout the Western world after the successful mission (Txillardegi,
1984). Other authors also have written science fiction, but it is
marginal in their literary career: José Muñoyerro's 1967 short story "Ilargian ere euskaraz hitz egiten da" (Basque Is Also Spoken

On The Moon) and Txomin Peillen's "Itzal gorria" (Red Shadow) written in 1972 are science fiction, but neither author is a specialist, as Iban Zaldua in his monograph about science fiction (Zaldua, 2018) calls the authors who dedicate their literary career to science fiction. Mayi Pelot is widely credited as the first specialist in science fiction written in Basque. In the 1990s and first decade of the 2000s, a large part of the production of the genre was aimed at children and young adults, but there are works for adults by authors whose main genre is not science fiction. Writers Iban Zaldua and Harkaitz Cano are outstanding examples. In 2004 Cano published *Belarraren ahoa* (The Edge of the Grass), based on the counterfactual premise that the Nazis won World War II and sent troops to the United States to invade it. In his 2005 *Etorkizuna* (Future), Zaldua revisits the past by mixing genres. More Basque writers are publishing science fiction with increasing success. Itxaro Borda, who had already published some science fiction stories with *Maiatz*, published *Kripton 85* in 2018, a novel written in 2012 in the wake of the Fukushima nuclear disaster, in which, from environmental and feminist perspectives, she reflects on the unsustainability of the capitalist system, forced migration, and human relations. Maite Darceles published *Bihotzean daramagun mundua* (The World We Carry in Our Hearts) in 2019, in which she explores the surveillance exercised through technology with an alternative society model. And lastly, literary projects like Zirriborroak eta gero, by the art space AZALA, is a virtual and multilingual initiative that calls on Basque authors to write speculative stories on present issues affecting the Basque Country.

Basque science fiction has received little critical attention. Zaldua (2018) hints at the possibility that, because most of its production is tagged as young adult literature, the genre may be perceived as infantile and, therefore, pushed into the background of literary criticism. Though it lacks the recognition and respect of more canonical literatures, that very lack grants greater freedom to the writer. Itxaro Borda explains: "When you are a writer on the periphery, you function aside from the literary turmoil; you are not in the eye of the storm. It means you enjoy more freedom of choice when it comes to topics, language, human relationships, and political opinions" (Alberdi, 2010). In essence, science fiction is fertile ground for authors and readers to ponder current social issues and speculate about possible consequences and alternative solutions without the cultural limitations of their time. In this aspect, there is plenty of room for science fiction to keep pushing the limits of Basque literature.

MAYI PELOT

Mayi Pelot (b. Talence, France, April 12, 1947) was the first Basque science fiction writer. Her publications span from only 1982 to 1992, but she is especially relevant for the genre because she laid the groundwork for future writers of science fiction.

She studied Greek, Latin, and French in college. After passing the teacher certification exam, she began working in a high school in Biarritz, NBC, teaching Latin, Greek, and French literatures. She was, therefore, proficient in Greek, Roman, and Norse mythology, and their influence is present throughout her work. Pelot's classic background is most noticeable in her poetry, where she interlaces oral literature and traditional classic literary references, and centers on themes such as death and love against a bucolic background.

For her science fiction influences, Pelot cites Ray Bradbury, first and foremost, for his aesthetics and his poetic use of the language; Isaac Asimov, for his fine ability to create an entire civilization in Foundation; Philip José Farmer, for his linguistic explorations and his reflections on religion, the soul, and sexuality as inherently human; Phillip K. Dick, for his audacious and daring ideas and dark humor; Michel Demuth, scientist and writer, for his determination to avoid English and Greek when creating new words, and for his peculiar use of eroticism in his work.

Pelot began her science fiction journey reading Ray Bradbury. She then went to Henday, NBC, to work, and found that her coworkers were avid readers of science fiction. One of them planned a lesson for their students, and they taught it together. She read several books in a short time to formulate her thoughts for the lessons, then joined the class in writing about what they read.

To the question "Why science fiction?" the Basque writer replies in her interview with Borda and Landa in 1986:

> It gives me the opportunity to explore exoticism; I am too well acquainted with today's Earth to do that in the here and now. The future is very interesting to me: it is the realm of possibility, of what could be done, except, of course, in the aftermath of a nuclear catastrophe. If an event of such a nature happened, there would be no future, nothing, no one. Science fiction lets you talk about today's most obvious and pressing issues, but it is also a space for much more, I think, where you can explore the consequences of the not so obvious problems of our time such as pollution or other social matters. I think fiction is a tool for analyzing those matters, to estimate their trajectory and uncover their consequences.

Pollution and nuclear energy are major points of concern in her work. She kept up with global and local events like the Iranian Revolution of 1979, the Cold War, and, as mentioned, the risks of nuclear plants in the Basque Country. Scientific developments like cloning, or disasters like the 1984 industrial explosion in Bhopal, India, were of extreme interest to her, too. In short, Pelot found her world a fantastic source of inspiration and ideas. She was intrigued by people, life, and death.

Mayi Pelot learned (unified) Basque at 23 in an attempt to feel closer to her country. She found that writing fiction was a place to practice and experiment with the language. She spoke several languages, which contributed to the linguistic richness of her work. She cared for the language she used in her stories and introduced a variety of neologisms mixing Basque, English, and French with Greek and Latin roots: ovamobile, hyperglass, robopol, galaxipol, among many others. (See the translator's note.) In the first four stories, because the NBC has been colonized by the United States of the World, Pelot adapts the names Euskal/Eskual Herri (current spelling of the Basque Country) and Bayonne as Esqwal Herry and New Byorn to possible English spellings.

Mayi Pelot, like the majority of Basque cultural activists and organizations in the 1980s, was worried about the state of the Northern Basque Country and was involved in the recovery and fostering of the Basque culture and language. She worked as an editor of a Basque-French bilingual dictionary, taught courses in the university of Bayonne and, at the local radio station, Gure Irratia, managed performances from play adaptations by Isaac Asimov and from operas by Richard Wagner.

She wrote multiple short stories and poems for *Maiatz*, and published three books, all of them in Basque: The first one was *Biharko oroitzapenak (Memories of Tomorrow)* (1985), then, in 1987, came the second one, *Teleamarauna,* which shares many elements with *Memories of Tomorrow,* as they are both set in the same galaxy and some of their characters have telepathic abilities. In *Teleamarauna,* however, telepathy becomes the main focus of the story, as an oppressed community uses it as a tool to rise against their oppressors. She published her third and last book *Hinduismoa, monoteismoa mila aurpegiduna* in 1992.

Mayi Pelot died on October 6, 2016, in Biarritz, Northern Basque Country. In the aftermath of her death, Basque feminists interested in science fiction by Basque authors have rediscovered her work and reintroduced it to the world. Pelot's life and work were discussed at the first occurrence of Bilbao's feminist science fiction festival AnsibleFest, and some of her stories can be listened to on the literature podcast Xerezaderen Artxiboa. Science fiction book clubs, too, spread across the country, serve as platforms for Basque feminist science fiction, where new voices come together with trailblazers like Pelot.

MEMORIES OF TOMORROW

Memories of Tomorrow, the first book published by Mayi Pelot, collects six stories that take place in the same galaxy but at different times. The first four happen in 2050 and the last two in the 3500s.

"Miren," "Row, Row," and "Feedback" only provide hints of the social, historical, and political background of this new Basque Country because they are meant to build momentum until the truth is uncovered in "The Digital Maze," a longer story where Pelot constructs a more elaborate plot and nuanced characters. All four stories provide a polyphonic account of the same event and take place in or are related to a Basque Country in the second half of the 21st century in the aftermath of WWIII. The Southern Basque Country was decimated by a nuclear accident and later became an uninhabitable desert. The Northern Basque Country, on the other hand, has expanded and gained influence across Europe. Basque is not an endangered language anymore; on the contrary, it has established itself as one of the main languages of the West. For the first time, the Basque Country plays a key role in the international arena. The world events of the 1980s, such as the Cold War between the USA and the USSR and the Iranian Revolution of 1979, are depicted as taking place in a world on the cusp of nuclear war. The United States of the World, Iran, Pakistan, China, and other mega-nations have invaded several countries of the world and are threatening each other with nuclear war. As the leaders of these nations advance in their warmongering goals by building weapons and defense strategies, the citizens of their colonized countries suffer the consequences of their practices.

In "Miren," we follow a woman through a critical afternoon in her life. Miren arrives at her house after work to prepare for going to a euthanasia center at the other end of the city. Throughout the story, Pelot presents us with a variety of technological devices: facial recognition cameras, individual driverless vehicles, virtual reality rooms. Sigma is mentioned for the first time, although briefly, as the company that operates most of the technological devices for public use. "Miren" introduces readers to the hyper-technologized society that the post-World War III Basque Country has become. The story models the harsh reality many Basque people face in Pelot's 2050, working precarious jobs near a toxic sea that result in their becoming terminally ill. Miren chooses to die when and how she wants to. Her last moments are suffused with images of traditional Basque rural life, including a shepherd dog, an eagle, the mountains, and Basque popular music.

In "Row, Row," a little girl called Leyre learns about the sea for the first time. After a teacher describes it as it is in the present and as it was in the 20th century, Leyre realizes that the sea made her aunt Miren sick.

The sea has a special meaning in the Basque collective imagination. It is an element surrounded by mythology and lore, and is a symbol of prosperity that brings food, industry, and commerce, and the possibility of knowing other lands. The sailing tradition goes back centuries in Basque history, from the whalers who traveled to the east coast of what is now Canada to the thousands of Basques who partook in the colonization of the Americas and, later in history, emigrated or went into exile there. The original title, "Boga-Boga," refers to a popular Basque song that talks about the sailors who have to leave the Basque Country for a far-away land and will no longer see the seaports of their hometowns again.

"Feedback" is set in Córdoba, Spain. In it, we learn about the fate of the Southern Basque Country, that the Islamic empire of Iran has colonized Spain as well as other countries, and that Iran has just lost India, a colony, to Pakistan. The leader, Reza, feels betrayed and seeks revenge. The Iranian leader wants to use the SBC as a site for his missiles and asks Nizam, the main character, for information.

The story depicts the call to prayer as robotized and technologized and how all the inhabitants, wherever they are, practice it for unity, brotherhood, and peace among the faithful. The story is laden with irony: While the entire population prays several times a day, the Iranian leader is only interested in accumulating power and land, and in going to war with other countries. Nizam, who is aware of the contradiction, provides an ironic viewpoint.

These three stories provide the corners of the puzzle in which the fourth story unfolds. Through three personal perspectives, the stories provide hints of the social, historical, and political background of this new Basque Country.

In "Telelaberintoa"("The Digital Maze"), Pelot paints a more complex and concrete reality. Anaiz is a Basque woman living in New York, the capital of the United States of the World, to work at Sigma's Temple of the Mind. The narrator describes Anaiz as a woman who longs for the simpler, less artificial way of life that her Basque hometown offers. But moving back to her hometown would entail sacrificing her New York job and life. And then one day, Sigma assigns her a job as an interpreter/guide in Byorn, NBC, where the company has established a colony of settlers.

The settlement in the city is bringing in wealthier people and driving out the native inhabitants. The locals have adapted to new forms of agriculture and begun selling produce to Sigma settlers. So few Basque natives remain that the hordes of tourists who visit the area learn about Basque culture and folklore from androids. Plus, the USW citizens living in Byorn, Anaiz's boss Jep Weber, for example, do not know their Basque neighbors and have no interest in knowing them. They view Basque culture and customs as atavistic and ignore Basques' intellectual and technological skills. Sigma and its settlers justify the actions they perpetrate against the locals (pushing them off their land or replacing them with androids, for example) by the supposed moral superiority of the Sigma settlers. In sum, Sigma casts Basques as other.

By becoming a Sigma member herself, Anaiz, too, has othered her own people. At first, Anaiz believes in her mission and trusts that Sigma and her boss have good intentions. One of Anaiz's new assignments is to convince her people that Sigma is planning to rid the city of pollution, although Sigma's real plan is to install a dome where only Sigmatians will be allowed. Her other assignment is to be a cultural and linguistic bridge between Jep Weber and the inhabitants of her town. Jep is a flat character who shows no signs of growth as the story develops. What makes him interesting is how he sees Anaiz, as a silly, malleable girl, unable to see beyond the surface. Through Anaiz, Jep is able to meet some of the locals, some of them very critical of Sigma, and assess the risks and challenges Sigma may be facing in the town. But as Anaiz reconnects with her past and her family and friends, she grows suspicious of Jep and begins to question her role as a settler. Finally, she discovers that the company is building a giant dome where Sigma settlers will take shelter and live through an imminent nuclear attack, while the locals will be left to die. Anaiz adopts the role that Malinalli (Malinche) played in Mexico with the Spanish and Basque colonizers and the Aztecs; or Sacagawea, on the Oregon trail with the English colonizers and Native American tribes. Both women were natives of the colonized land and witnesses of the destruction of their people, and were used for the benefit and interest of the colonizers. But, unlike Malinalli and Sacagawea, Anaiz acts from a position of privilege: she is employed by Sigma and not enslaved by it, which means Anaiz is able to make choices. After she finds out about Sigma's real plans, Anaiz joins the anti-Sigma movement and decides to break ties with the company.

Anaiz is a complex character who experiences internal struggles. She is at a crossroads between a life that provides her with wealth and prestige as an individual and a life that strives for collective thriving as a community. She also struggles to find her place and voice in a world ruled by men. Her boss Jep Weber tells her what to say and what to keep secret; Gorka challenges her understanding of Sigma and her identity as a Basque person and a settler. In the end, Anaiz is the only character who holds enough pieces of the puzzle to see the greater picture, but she unfortunately lacks the power to change things.

Like Anaiz, many of Pelot's leading characters are female, a not so common characteristic of the Basque literature of the time. These characters are determined and reflective: Miren's range of action is limited, but she refuses to be passive; she owns her own body and chooses to control her own destiny. Leyre brings hope for a better, more conscientious future. She is new to the world but already inquisitive and critical. And Anaiz is a complex woman who experiences power and oppression simultaneously.

For environmentalists, Mayi Pelot's book is a clear call to action. She denounces the unequal distribution of wealth and natural resources and delivers a stern warning about the risks of nuclear energy. The Southern Basque Country has turned into a desert, and the sea is blocked off from the land by a wall and has become a health threat.

An Orwellian atmosphere pervades all four stories. The European countries under the rule of the United States of the World are openly run by Sigma, which may be characterized as a light version of "Big Brother." In the territories under the rule of Iran, technology is used for call to prayer and meditation in both private and public spaces.

While Pelot does give some space to the leaders of the mega nations, (Reza, Sha, Opusdey, Hito, Gandhi), their voices speak in the background. The author chooses to focus on the lives of characters who have little power to change the impending chaos and yet decide to take action, even if it is to their own demise.

Ultimately, what worries Mayi Pelot are the consequences that colonialism and imperialistic wars cause in society: poverty, oppression, environmental degradation, inequality, and gentrification, among others. Regardless of the system it imposes—capitalism or socialism in the case of *Memories of Tomorrow*—colonialism is detrimental to the colonized and has as its main objective benefitting the colonizing country.

In the next two stories, "Choppy Water" and "The Exchange," Pelot takes a big leap in time and transports us to other planets. These last two stories are characterized by their exoticism. Pelot uses colorful and evocative descriptions. Inventing new worlds gives her the opportunity to unleash her creativity.

"Choppy Water," in the words of the author, is a completely different story:

It takes place in a fantasy world, with its own problems and civilizations. It is a political story and a poem laced together. Unemployment is high, there is no construction of houses, they use water channels instead of roads, and technology is very present in their lives. The city suffers earthquakes every day. It is not a patriarchal system, doctors have moral issues, and cloning and euthanizing individuals is a normal practice. (Borda & Landa, 1986)

This story has more than one main character, all intertwined, passing the baton from one to another. The first one is Katryl, a fugitive from the city of Deunargi, in Neobaskia, a territory on the planet Turion that was conquered and divided by the Basik and Kobol planets eight centuries earlier. This is in clear reference to the situation of the Basque Country, split between Spain and France. The natural resources of Neobaskia are being exploited for war purposes, and the natives who fight against this situation have to go into exile or suffer lethal consequences. There is a drive and determination in the characters of "Choppy Water" that resemble the Basque society of the 1980s and its relentless fight to secure a future and a voice in an increasingly globalized world.

In this new era, technology is applied to police practices. An hallucinogenic drug originating on Earth is used on detainees, and android policemen have weapons in their foreheads.

In his flight, Katryl reaches the city of Shuripi, where he meets with more Neobaskia people and shares memories about others who have lost their lives in the fight. Water and Shuripi are relevant characters in the story, just as much as Katryl is. The atmosphere is damp, dark, fragile, and decaying. Thanks to Pelot's graphic descriptions and poetic style, one can almost hear the rain dropping and the water splashing. Regardless of its flaws, Shuripi radiates a sense of coziness, inclusivity, and belonging, and, at the end, it nourishes hope.

While in the city, Katryl falls in love with Zerune, the leading voice of the second part of the story. Through the eyes of Zerune, we discover Shuripi's underground. In the quote above, Pelot mentions that the characters in "Choppy Water" do not operate by the rules of the patriarchal system, but the story suggests otherwise. Female characters have no space for public activism as male characters do. In the fight to free their people from Basik and Kobol, the network of women Zerune belongs to plays a crucial role, but it functions in the shadows. The work of these women is completely invisible to even the men of Neobaskia. In the beginning, we learn that the key to the survival of their people is that the galactic laws protect the territories of more than five million inhabitants. The women's plan is to clone deceased male activists in order to maintain the population above five million, and to perpetuate their ideology and their fight. They raise their children as their ancestors did a long time ago. Like Basque nationalist women in the "Basque conflict," the female characters of this story are the caretakers, widows, and mothers of patriotic men.

Mayi Pelot ends her book with "The Exchange." She categorizes it as a space opera, and quite literally it is an adaptation of Richard Wagner's *Siegfried* that happens in space. It recounts the story of God Wotan and Goddess Erda, but with a twist, as the author explains: "Erda, a very passive character in the original story, becomes an increasingly smart and quite extravagant character in mine" (Borda & Landa, 1986). In this story, we can see Pelot mixing classic literature and mythology with Hinduism. Erda symbolizes a higher level of consciousness and Wotan the pupil who wishes to achieve it with the help of Erda's Norns, a form of guide.

The atmosphere in "The Exchange" comes in stark contrast to the previous stories. It is a story that ponders life as we know it and life as we would want it to be, and the possibility of finding one's true self and reconnecting with the world through it. It is written in a hopeful and freeing language: sensual, colorful, and intimist. It is prose poetry. The imagery is bright and peaceful, like a bucolic scene from a Renaissance painting or the garden of Eden. All the elements—nature, bodies, minds, smells, emotions—contribute to its main ideal: full understanding of ourselves and what surrounds us.

In this reinterpretation of *Siegfried*, Wotan's powers lie in his technological competencies. He is the president of several companies, a pilot of ships, and a warrior, and his semi-mortality is the product of technological advances. These superficial accomplishments do not bring him happiness, and he regrets not having a deeper connection with his children and wife. Wotan feels a great existential emptiness. Erda, by contrast, is an ethereal being, a sort of omnipotent collective consciousness that lives underground.

At a certain point, Wotan and Erda start communicating via computer messages, and he decides to go to Daleth to meet her. The story depicts the relationship that arises from that encounter. Wotan does not know how to communicate with Erda, but she gives him instructions on how to do so. He gradually opens up to Erda, sharing the most intimate aspects of his life and reconsidering his past actions. When he has fully exposed his truth to Erda, Wotan finally connects with the collective and all-powerful consciousness that she is. By examining Wotan's life and identity, Pelot places a mirror in front of the reader and asks them to examine the values and fears of our society. In the end, Wotan returns to the human world but is left with two reminders of his experience: the loss of one eye, the price of his communication with Erda, and a daughter, Brünhilde, with whom he can communicate telepathically.

Children are bits of optimism and hope that break with the dystopian atmosphere of *Memories of Tomorrow*. All of the children in these stories represent a new beginning: Leyre and the little kid in the dome witness atrocities, but because of their reaction, we are left with the hope that when they grow older, they will explore the causes of the events they witnessed. The cloned children of Shuripi will keep Neobaskia alive, and they will be raised within a conscientious network of people aware of their responsibility towards their natural and social environments; and Brünhilde will be raised by the traditional methods of an ancient civilization but by two women, Fricka and Erda. Eventually, she will become a powerful leader by taking the place of her dad at the front of Wallhall. But the hope that these children may bring to the world is only made possible by the invisible work carried out by women. In "Choppy Water," reproduction and parenting are part of a secret underground plan hidden from all men; in "The Exchange," Fricka raises her and Wotan's children on her own, but earns no recognition for it, and in the rest of the stories reproductive work is barely mentioned.

In essence, *Memories of Tomorrow* is a poignant political commentary on the oppressive systems that rule our world and their practices of othering, neocolonialism, gentrification, and massive exploitation of natural resources. Pelot often focuses her lens on the individuals and communities that are oppressed by the policies and actions of oppressive governments and points to the relationship with nature and one another as a healthy, sustainable alternative to our current world structure. The universe she created as the background for these stories is just as relevant in her work. The insertion of traditional elements, like the goat milk Katryl drinks in "Choppy Water" or Gorka's wooden house-door in "The Digital Maze," into highly technologized spaces creates a home-like atmosphere in a very hostile environment. The use of color in her descriptions of places and characters like the main hall where Miren goes at the end of the story or the way Zerune is described, brightens otherwise grim scenarios. Her storytelling is dynamic and concise, conveying precious information in very short stories like "Miren" or "Row, Row." All in all, *Memories of Tomorrow* collects a set of vibrant and enigmatic visions that emanated from one of the most creative minds of contemporary Basque literature.

Sources

THE BASQUE COUNTRY

Agirre Dorronsoro, L., and Eskisabel Larrañaga, I. (2019). *Trikua esnatu da: euskaratik feminismora eta feminismotik euskarara.* Susa.

Gandarias, Z. (2019). "Basque Women in Exile: Remembering their Voices and Impact in Literature through the Cultural Magazine Euzko-Gogoa." *Memory and Emotion: Women's Stories.* http://works.bepress.com/ziortza-gandariasbeldarrain/4/

López Romo, Raúl (2008). "Tiñendo la patria de verde y violeta. La relación del nacionalismo vasco radical con los movimientos antinuclear y feminista en la transición." *University of the Basque Country*, 124.

Wikipedia contributors. (2021, September). "Basque Country (greater region)." *Wikipedia, The Free Encyclopedia.* https://en.wikipedia.org/w/index.php?title=Basque_Country_(greater_region)&oldid=1044539090

BASQUE LITERATURE AND MAIATZ

Alberdi Albeniz, Uxue (2010, October). "Betidanik idatzi dut lesbiana izateaz." *Argia.* www.argia.eus/argia-astekaria/2230/itxaro-borda

Aldekoa Beitia, I. (2012). "Una mirada a la literatura vasca y a la postmodernidad." *Oihenart*, 27, 9-25.

Borda, I. (1989). *Emakumeak idazle: Antologia eta ohar zenbait.* Txertoa.

——. (2007, September). "Maiatz, 25 urte." *Bazka.* Itsasoa Ontzian. www.bazka.info/?p=227

Britannica, The Editors of Encyclopaedia. (2021, January). "François Mitterrand." *Encyclopedia Britannica.* https://www.britannica.com/biography/Francois-Mitterrand. Accessed 19 September 2021

Etxezaharreta, L. (2002). "Euskarazko literatura Iparraldean XXI. mende atarian." *Maiatz.* 661-666.

Gabilondo, J. (2000). "Itxaro Borda: Melancholic Migrancy And The Writing Of A National Lesbian Self." *Asju.* Xxxiv-2, 291-314.

——. (1998). "Del exilio materno a la utopía personal: Política cultural en la narrativa vasca de mujeres." *Ínsula.* 623, 32-36.

Lasarte, G. (2013). "Genero Eta Sexuaren Berridazketa: Itxaro Borda Eta Polizia Eleberrien Kasua." *Euskera.* 58, 2. 753-783.

Olaziregi Alustiza, María José. (n.d.) "Narrativa Vasca Del Siglo Xx: Una Narrativa Con Futuro." University of the Basque Country. *Basque Literature Portal.* http://www.basqueliterature.com/basque/historia/hogeimende/narratiba/eleberria

Urkiza, A. (2006). *Zortzi unibertso, zortzi idazle.* Alberdania.

Urkulo Rodríguez, I. (2012). "Euskal narratiba XXI. mendean: emakumeak idazle." *Oihenart,* 27, 201-233.

BASQUE SCIENCE FICTION

Euskadi Irratia (2019, November). "Itxaro Bordarekin kronika eraikitzeko eta espekulatzeko fikzioaz." *Arratsean.* https://www.eitb.eus/eu/irratia/euskadi-irratia/programak/arratsean/osoa/6801906/itxaro-borda-susmaezinak-eta-kripton-85-nobelez- arratseaneuskadi-irratia/

Sarriugarte Mochales, D. (2019, October). "Arrate Hidalgo: 'Baztertutako identitateek betidanik idatzi dute zientzia fikzioa.'" *Uberan.* http://uberan.eus/?gatzetan-gordeak/elkarrizketak/item/arrate-hidalgo-baztertutako-identitateek-betidanik-idatzi-dute-zientzia-fikzioa

Txillardegi, José Luis Alvarez Esperanza. (1984, June). "Lau ipuin hauen inguru-giroaz." *Donostia Euskaraz.* http://www.donostiaeuskaraz.eus/donostia/idazleak/liburuak/gehi/0001302.htm

Ugarte Irizar, I. (2018, July). "Distopia bat orainaren hurren." *Berria.* https://www.berria.eus/paperekoa/1893/028/001/2018-07- 19/distopia_bat_orainaren_hurren.htm

Villarreal, Mariano. (2021, September). "Basque SF." *The Encyclopedia of Science Fiction.* Eds. John Clute, David Langford, Peter Nicholls and Graham Sleight. Gollancz. http://www.sf-encyclopedia.com/entry/basque_sf

Zaldua, I. (2018). "Zientzia fikzioa monografikoa." *HEGATS, 32,* 45-87.

Zirriborroak eta gero (n.d.). https://borradoresdelfuturo.net/?lang=eu

MAYI PELOT

Ansible Fest (n.d.). *Zientzia-fikzio feministaren jaialdia.* https://ansiblefest.wordpress.com/

Martín Alegre, S. (2010). "Mujeres en la literatura de ciencia ficción: Entre la escritura y el feminismo." *Dossiers Feministes*, *14*, 108-128.

Pelot, M. (2019). *mayi pelot. olerki, ipuin eta eleberriak*. Maiatz.

Sarriugarte Mochales, D. (2019, March). "Mayi Pelot, gure zientzia fikzioaren aitzindari." *Argia*. https://www.argia.eus/argia-astekaria/2636/mayi-pelot

Unanue Irureta, M. (2019, September). "Zientzia fikzioa egiten duten andreak 'rara avis' gisan tratatzen dituzte." *Berria*. https://www.berria.eus/paperekoa/1886/040/001/2019-09-10/zientzia- fikzioa-egiten-duten-andreak-rara-avis-gisan-tratatzen-dituzte.htm

MEMORIES OF TOMORROW

Borda, I., and J. Landa. (1986, November). "Mayi Pelotekin solasean: 'Gure planeta mendurarendako ezagunegia delako idazten dut zientzia fikzioa'" *Susa*. https://andima.armiarma.eus/susa/susa1718.htm

Galarraga, Aritz (2013, June). "Bakan ale bitxia" *Kritiken hemeroteka*. https://kritikak.armiarma.eus/?p=5851

Various authors. Reviews of *Memories of Tomorrow*. https://zubitegia.armiarma.eus/?i=118

Various authors. (2019, July). "Mayi Peloten Zientzia Fikzioa: Miren, Boga-boga, Feedback." *Xerezaderen Artxiboa*. https://xerezade.org/irakurketa/mayi-peloten-zientzia-fikzioa-miren-boga-boga-feedback

Translator Biography

Arrate Hidalgo (Bilbao, 1987) is a translator, editor, and cultural agent based in Bilbao. With a background in English and Medieval literature, she has been an Associate Editor of Aqueduct Press since 2015. After eight years living and working between the UK and USA, she returned to her native Basque Country in 2017. Since then she has embarked on various projects to communicate and develop non-hegemonic visions of the future: she co-founded the feminist SF festival AnsibleFest and co-created the podcast "¿Qué haría Barbarella?", and she currently organizes sci-fi-themed bertsolarism (sung improvised poetry) sessions with women bertsolaris, as well as coordinates the editorial project *Zirriborroak eta gero/Borradores del futuro*, a series of chapbooks envisioning desirable futures of existing social/community initiatives in the Basque sociopolitical context. Mayi Pelot's *Memories of Tomorrow* is her first full-length book solo translation project from Basque into English.

Author Biography

Mayi Pelot (Talence, 1947-Biarritz, 2016) is recognized as one of the first authors to have written science fiction as a genre in Basque. Having pursued French, Latin, and Greek studies in college, she later on became a school teacher in Biarritz, where she learned Basque. She was an active member of the Basque-speaking literary and linguistic community, co-founding the literary magazine *Maiatz*, presenting radio shows based on Asimov's and Wagner's works in the first years of the Basque-speaking radio station Gure Irratia, and participating in the development of the *Nola erran* French-Basque dictionary, launched by the Public Office of the Basque Language. A lover of music from around the world and a devout yoga practitioner, she wrote a book-length essay on Hinduism on top of her poetry and fiction. This, in 1992, would be her last publication. She adopted a son and led a private life until her death of cancer on October 6, 2016.